**Marsh cau**
**that could**
**He change**
**seconds later, the dark car behind them**
**changed lanes, too.**

He tightened his grip and hit the gas. At the last minute, he yanked the steering wheel to get off the interstate.

"What's going on?" Stacy asked.

"There's someone behind us." He quickly pulled his phone from his pocket and handed it to her. "Call Jackson. Tell him we need help."

The black car once again appeared in his rearview mirror. There was no mistaking the driver's intent as the vehicle behind them closed the gap.

"Jackson! We need help!" Stacy's voice was panicked as she provided their location. "Hurry."

At least on the highway Marsh could drive faster without endangering Stacy's safety more than he already was.

After a long moment, he thought he'd lost the dark vehicle. But then it appeared behind them.

Only this time, the driver went into the right-hand lane. Marsh grimly realized the intent was to come up along Stacy's side of the car.

"Get down!" He slammed his foot on the accelerator as the driver of the dark car lowered his window, revealing a gun...

**Laura Scott** has always loved romance and read faith-based books by Grace Livingston Hill in her teenage years. She's thrilled to have been given the opportunity to retire from thirty-eight years of nursing to become a full-time author. Laura has published over thirty books for Love Inspired Suspense. She has two adult children and lives in Milwaukee, Wisconsin, with her husband of thirty-five years. Please visit Laura at laurascottbooks.com, as she loves to hear from her readers.

### Books by Laura Scott

#### Love Inspired Suspense

*Hiding in Plain Sight*
*Amish Holiday Vendetta*
*Deadly Amish Abduction*
*Tracked Through the Woods*
*Kidnapping Cold Case*
*Guarding His Secret Son*

#### Texas Justice

*Texas Kidnapping Target*
*Texas Ranger Defender*
*Dangerous Texas Secrets*

#### Mountain Country K-9 Unit

*Baby Protection Mission*

#### Dakota K-9 Unit

*Chasing a Kidnapper*

Visit the Author Profile page at LoveInspired.com for more titles.

# DANGEROUS TEXAS SECRETS

## LAURA SCOTT

**LOVE INSPIRED SUSPENSE**
INSPIRATIONAL ROMANCE

MIX
Paper | Supporting responsible forestry
FSC® C021394
www.fsc.org

# LOVE INSPIRED® SUSPENSE
INSPIRATIONAL ROMANCE

Recycling programs for this product may not exist in your area.

ISBN-13: 978-1-335-95752-8

Dangerous Texas Secrets

Love Inspired
22 Adelaide St. West, 41st Floor
Toronto, Ontario M5H 4E3, Canada
www.LoveInspired.com

HarperCollins Publishers
Macken House, 39/40 Mayor Street Upper,
Dublin 1, D01 C9W8, Ireland
www.HarperCollins.com

**Printed in Lithuania**

Jesus saith unto him, I am the way, the truth, and the life: no man cometh unto the Father, but by me.
—*John* 14:6

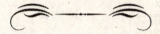

This book is dedicated with love to my daughter Nicole Collins. May God bless you and keep you all the days of your life.

# ONE

Battling a wave of exhaustion, Stacy Copeland drove her SUV into the garage of the small home she owned just outside of San Antonio, Texas. Her widow support group meeting had gone longer than planned and at six months pregnant, nine thirty at night was well past her usual bedtime.

As she closed the garage door behind her against the chilly February wind and pushed out of the car, she wondered if she'd ever get used to coming home to an empty house. Almost three months ago now, her husband Dan had been shot and killed at an ATM machine in what the San Antonio Police were calling a robbery gone bad. They hadn't even been married a full year.

Now she'd be raising their daughter, alone.

She rounded the back of the SUV, deciding not to grab her laptop from the back seat, then paused. The corner of the rug in front of the door leading into the house was folded over. Tiny hairs prickled along the back of her neck.

It hadn't been like that when she'd left. She remembered the rug was flat because she'd dropped her keys and had to finagle her pregnant body down to the ground to retrieve them. She would have noticed the curled corner and fixed it so she wouldn't trip and potentially hurt herself or her baby.

Was she losing her mind? Stacy took a step back, shivering. Had she kicked up the corner of the rug without realizing it? She was far enough along that she couldn't really see her own feet.

She listened intently but didn't hear anything.

Telling herself not to be foolish, she hiked her purse strap over her shoulder and moved forward. It was late. She was exhausted. Her mind was playing tricks on her.

She pushed the door open and stepped across the threshold. As she turned to shut the door behind her, a man grabbed her from behind, yanking her against his hard body. The cold sharp edge of a knife pressed painfully against her throat.

"Give me the code," he hissed.

Paralyzed with fear, her heart raced. How had he gotten inside? Who was he? What code?

"Now!" He pressed the edge of the knife into her skin. She could feel the trickle of blood running down her neck.

He was going to kill her! And her baby!

"What code?" she asked hoarsely.

"The one your husband stole," he growled. She couldn't see her assailant's face. His breath reeked of cigarette smoke and greasy fries. Her stomach churned with nausea as she tried to gather her fractured thoughts.

Dan had stolen a code? Was that the real reason he'd been murdered?

A fresh wave of fear washed over her. She didn't know anything about a code!

"Hurry," the guy said. "Or I'll kill you and keep looking for myself."

"I—I remember now. I-it's hidden in the office," she stammered, fumbling in her coat pocket for her key fob. When he loosened his grip so they could move toward the office, she hit the panic alarm.

The assailant loosened his grip and spun toward the sound of the car alarm. Stacy broke free and bolted across the kitchen toward the bedrooms located down the hall. In some portion of her mind, she realized the house had been ransacked.

Had the assailant found her gun? The one her Texas Ranger brother Tucker had purchased for her?

The assailant lunged forward and grabbed the hem of her flannel maternity shirt. She rounded on him, lashing out with her foot the way Tuck had taught her. Somehow she managed to connect with his groin, causing him to double over in pain.

Swallowing a sob, she darted past him, deciding against finding her gun. She needed to get out of here! She raced down the hall to the laundry room and out the door leading to her backyard.

The car alarm was still blaring loudly. She cut through the backyard to reach her neighbor. Slamming her fist against the Feldmans' door, she screamed. "Help! Help me!"

It felt like forever before Hank Feldman opened the back door. "Stacy? What's going on?"

"Please help me." She pushed past him into the house. "There's a man in my house with a knife. He—" she put a hand to the cut along her throat "—he threatened to kill me."

"Call 911 and wait here." Hank was in his sixties, but that didn't stop him from grabbing his shotgun.

"No, don't." She grabbed his arm. "I don't want you to be hurt."

"Call 911," Hank repeated. "I'm just going to check the place out."

Before she could say more, Hank disappeared outside with his shotgun. Staggering into the kitchen, she sank into the closest chair as her legs threatened to buckle beneath her. Rummaging through her purse, she pulled out her phone.

"This is 911. Please provide the address you're calling from," the dispatcher said.

"My address is 210 Sunflower Lane. My name is Stacy Copeland. There's a man with a knife in my house." She could hardly believe she was saying the words out loud. "Please hurry."

"Are you safe?" the dispatcher asked.

"Yes, I was able to get to my neighbor's. Just hurry!"

"I have two squads responding to your location," the dispatcher replied. "Please stay on the line."

"I can't." She ended the call, her fingers trembling so badly she almost dropped the phone. She needed help beyond the man with the knife.

She called Tuck, but he didn't answer. She thumbed the screen to find Marshall Branson's number. Marsh and Tucker were Texas Rangers. Marsh had gotten in touch with her after learning about Dan's murder, offering his support. They'd gotten close when they'd spent some time together at the Rocking T Ranch last September.

Back when her life was normal. Routine. The exact opposite of now.

"Stacy? What's wrong?" Marsh asked.

Tears welled in her eyes at the concern in his tone. "There was a man waiting in my house when I got home. He—held a knife to my throat. I—he wants some code that he claims Dan stole from him." She began to sob. "I don't know what he's talking about, Marsh. I don't know anything about a code!"

"Where are you now?" Marsh asked.

"I'm at my neighbor Hank Feldman's house. The police are on their way, too." She swiped at her eyes, trying to regain some semblance of control. "Marsh, I'm scared. What if he comes back? I think he looked for the code before I got home but didn't find it. He threatened to kill me and keep looking for it himself if I didn't hand it over."

"I'm on my way. Stay close to Hank until I can get there." She heard Marsh's car engine roaring to life and immediately felt better. "Don't go anywhere until I arrive."

"Okay. Thank you." She lowered her phone and took several deep breaths. Stress wasn't good for the baby.

Neither was being held at knifepoint.

She dropped her chin to her chest and took deep breaths. What was going on? Had her deceased husband really stolen something?

It seemed unlikely. They weren't rich. Without Dan's life insurance she'd have been out on the street. She'd used the money from his policy to refinance the house so that she could make the monthly mortgage payments on her salary alone.

If Dan had stolen something of value, where was it? Not in their bank account, that was for sure.

She wanted to believe this was a big misunderstanding. That the man with the knife had the wrong house. The wrong woman. The wrong husband.

But deep down, she knew the truth. Dan had been upset and edgy the last few weeks prior to his murder. So much so, that she'd wondered what had happened to the easygoing guy she'd married. Stacy had even considered the possibility he was having an extramarital affair.

Now she had to face the fact that her husband had stolen something important enough that a man with a knife had broken into her home.

Threatening to kill her and their unborn child.

Sick with dread, she lifted her gaze to the ceiling and prayed. *Lord Jesus, please protect me and my daughter!*

Texas Ranger Marshall Branson had just returned from a weeklong trip in Houston supporting the DEA in a massive drug bust. But the moment he'd heard Stacy's frightened voice, he'd thrown himself behind the wheel of his SUV and broke every highway speed limit to reach her small home on the northeast side of San Antonio.

Okay, maybe he had a soft spot for his buddy Tucker's younger sister. They'd gotten to know each other back in September when he'd stayed on the family ranch to protect Stacy and her grandfather when Tucker had found himself knee deep in danger. Since then, Stacy had lost her husband a month or so after discovering she was pregnant. Marshall had offered her his support, which she hadn't requested until now.

Two San Antonio squads were in the driveway of her house when he pulled up. Marsh raked his gaze over the scene as he slid out from behind the wheel.

"Who are you?" A uniformed officer strode toward

him, his hand resting on the butt of his weapon. His name tag read Wilson.

"Texas Ranger Branson." He gestured to the star on his leather jacket. "I'm a friend of the victim."

"I need you to stay back from the scene." Officer Wilson frowned, clearly concerned that Marsh was there to steal the case away. Which, to be fair, was true. Marsh wasn't sure what was going on, but the request for Stacy to hand over a stolen code was worrisome and he wasn't about to leave this to the locals.

A code to what? A lockbox? A storage unit? A bank account? The possibilities were endless.

Ignoring the cop's directive to stay back, he headed up the driveway. Based on the way the house to the left of Stacy's was lit up brighter than a Christmas tree, he veered toward it.

As he approached the front door, it opened. Stacy rushed out and threw herself into his arms.

"Marsh. I'm so happy to see you." Her words were muffled against his chest.

"Hey, don't worry. I'll keep you safe." He held her close for a long moment, then eased her back so he could see her face. "You're not hurt?"

"No. It's just a scratch." She lifted her hand to her neck. Seeing the bloody cut across her ivory skin was a kick to his gut. Fighting back his anger, he turned to glance back at her house. It didn't appear as if the local cops had anyone in custody.

"Thanks for coming." She attempted to smile but failed miserably. "I tried Tuck, but he didn't answer."

"Tuck is on a case in Austin." He put his arm around her slim shoulders and nudged her toward the door. "Let's go inside where it's warm. Have the police interviewed you, yet? Do they have any leads?"

"Yes, I spoke to a Detective Graves." She entered the house and gestured toward the living room. "Hank told me to make myself at home. He's still talking with the police."

Marsh intended to confer with the cops, too, but first he wanted to hear her side of the story. He dropped beside her on the sofa. "Can you tell me what happened?"

She nodded, tucking a strand of her long dark hair behind her ear. "I came home later than normal from my support group." She made a face. "Not sure why I bothered to go, it's not that helpful. There's an older man named Harold Green who seems to need people to talk to. Anyway, after getting out of the car, I noticed a corner of the rug in front of the door was curled up but told myself it was nothing. But the minute I stepped inside the house, a man grabbed me from behind and held a knife at my throat." She lifted her wide blue eyes to his. "He demanded I give him the code. The code my husband stole."

He nodded and reached for her hands. They were ice cold, so he covered them with his. "I'm sorry you had to go through that. What happened next?"

"He kept asking for the code, telling me he'd kill me if I didn't help him. I finally told him it was hidden in the office and hit the panic button on my key fob. That made him relax his grip and jerk toward the garage. I made a run for it. He grabbed the tail of my shirt and I kicked him in the—" She faltered, then continued, "He doubled over in pain. I rushed past him through the laundry room to get outside and ran here." She stared down at their entwined hands. "Hank let me in, told me to call 911 and ran over to my place with his shotgun. After calling the police, I contacted you."

"I'm glad." Marsh winced at the thought of her neighbor heading over to confront the guy by himself. A knife could be just as lethal as a gun. "I didn't see anyone in custody."

"No. Apparently he took off when I escaped." She frowned. "I wish they'd have caught him, though. I'm afraid he'll come back."

There was no doubt in Marsh's mind the perp would be back, possibly with additional reinforcements. "Don't worry, I'm taking you out of here as soon as you pack a bag." He glanced at her gently rounded stomach. Anyone who could threaten a pregnant woman was lower than scum. "I'm off duty for the next few days. You can stay with me until we know more about what's going on."

"I hate to put you out," she protested.

"Don't be silly. I'm only taking over what Tuck would do if he were here." Marsh briefly considered taking Stacy to the ranch, then decided against it.

"I won't go to the ranch," she said, as if reading his mind. "Tucker's wife, Leanne, is there and so is Pops. I don't want either of them to be in danger."

"I agree, that's not an option. This guy may know about the Rocking T." It wasn't a secret that Stacy and Tucker had grown up on their grandparents' ranch.

The sound of a door opening had Marsh jumping to his feet. He relaxed when an older man entered through the back door with a shotgun. "You must be Hank." Marsh stepped forward and extended his hand. "I'm Marshall Branson. A friend of Stacy's brother, Tucker."

"You're a ranger, too, I see." Hank nodded at the badge

on his chest as he shook his hand. "Glad you're here to help Stacy out. The guy who broke in did a number on her place. Messed it up bad." Hank glanced at Stacy. "You're welcome to stay here for as long as you need. I can make up the guest room for you."

"Thanks, but that won't be necessary. I'm taking Stacy someplace safe." Marsh was touched by Hank's willingness to help his neighbor. "We're going to pick up a few of her things, then hit the road."

"That's probably for the best," Hank agreed. "I won't worry as much knowing Stacy is with you."

Marsh nodded, then turned to offer Stacy a hand. She took it and allowed him to help her to her feet. He glanced back at Hank. "Have the police finished clearing the scene?"

"For the most part." Hank shrugged. "Stacy said the guy was wearing gloves. Doubt they'll bother searching for prints."

Marsh scowled but held his tongue. As much as he wanted to take over the investigation, his first concern was getting Stacy settled someplace safe. "Thanks again for being here when Stacy needed you."

"Anytime." Hank waved a hand. "Y'all be careful out there."

"Will do." Marsh escorted Stacy to the front door. "Thanks again."

Outside, they made their way across the yard to her house. The officers were discussing things off to the side but didn't stop them from entering the home. The garage door was open now and she headed inside.

"He must have gotten into the garage," she said almost as if talking to herself. "I noticed the corner of the rug was kicked up, so he must have come in this way. I just don't know how."

"You keep the garage service door locked?" he asked.

"Always. I rarely use it in the winter." She glanced at him. "It's creepy to know how easily he broke in. That he searched the place while I was gone."

"I know." Marsh could see the revulsion on her features at the idea of the knife-wielding man going through her things. "Let's grab a bag."

Stacy opened the door to the house and stepped inside. Gauging by how the color drained from her face, he could tell she was reliving the moment the perp grabbed her. He moved forward and took her hand.

"You're safe with me. Do you have a small suitcase?" He kept his tone calm and reassuring. "You'll feel better once we're out of here."

"Yes." She straightened her shoulders with a determination he admired and headed down the hall to her bedroom. "This will only take a moment."

Hank was right about the mess. While the living room and kitchen had been searched, most of the destruction was centered on the office. It was, after all, the most logical place to find a hidden code.

To what? He knew Dan worked for a tech company, as did Stacy. Could it be a computer code? The mystery nagged at him as he hovered in the doorway waiting for Stacy to pack her suitcase. When she finished, he stepped forward to take it from her.

"Wait. I'd like my laptop, too." She frowned. "I had left it in my car since I was going to need it for work. Tomorrow is a day I'm supposed to go to the office."

He hesitated, then shrugged. "Sure. We can take it

with us. But you'll have to let your boss know you're not going in."

"I know." She didn't look happy about that.

Marsh followed her to the garage. She opened her back passenger door and grabbed the computer case. He took that from her, too.

"We'll use my car, yours is registered under your name," he said. "It's better we don't have any connection to your home address since this guy knows where you live."

She grimaced, nodded and continued through the garage. He lengthened his stride to reach the SUV first. He paused to open the front passenger seat for her, then stashed the suitcase and computer in the back.

Joining her in the car, he started the engine, giving it a moment to warm up since Stacy was huddling in her seat. The temperature wasn't too bad, forty-five degrees, so he wasn't sure if she was physically cold or just still shaken from the assault. He backed out of her driveway.

"I wish there was a way to convince that man I don't know anything about their missing code." She glanced at him. "I hate knowing he'll come back."

Marsh's heart ached for her. "Can you remember anything else about him? Anything that might help us find him?"

"His breath reeked of cigarettes and greasy fries." She rubbed a hand over her belly as if to calm herself. Or the baby.

Maybe both.

"I know that doesn't help," she said with a sigh. "It all happened so fast. I got the impression he wasn't that tall, not like you and Tucker. Maybe five nine or five ten? He was on the lean side, sort of wiry, although he crumpled to the ground when I kicked him."

"That's good, Stacy. Anything else? Race?"

She frowned. "White, but with darker skin. Maybe mixed race? I can't be sure. I was too focused on getting away."

"Hey, don't stress." He reached out to pat her knee. "Every little detail helps."

"Because he wore gloves, the police don't think they'll find any prints or DNA." She sighed. "I wish I had thought of scratching him with my fingernails."

"You got away from him, that's what matters." Marsh gently squeezed her knee. "Please don't worry. We'll figure this out."

"Will we?" She turned to face him. "How? We don't know anything about him or the stupid code!"

A pair of headlights growing brighter in the rear view mirror caught his attention. Placing both hands on the wheel, he increased his speed.

The car behind them kept pace.

Not good. He considered his options. None were great, considering this stretch of road didn't have many cross streets.

"What's wrong?" Stacy glanced fearfully behind them. "Is that the knife man behind us?"

"I don't know. Hang on." He hit the gas again, sending the SUV surging forward. He managed to gain some distance but instinctively knew it wasn't enough.

He yanked the wheel hard to the right, tapping the brake slightly as they drove off the road and onto the frozen farmland. The move caught the other vehicle by surprise, giving them the advantage.

Until he heard the sharp report of gunfire. "Down!" he told Stacy. "Get down!"

Despite the uneven terrain, Marsh stomped on the accelerator, pushing the SUV as fast as possible to avoid being hit.

Or, worse, killed.

# TWO

The sharp crack of gunfire sent Stacy's heart into her throat. The SUV rocked from side to side over the uneven turf as Marsh drove across an open field. When he'd told her to get down, she bent over in her seat as much as she could, cradling her abdomen with one arm while gripping the armrest with the other to keep from being tossed around like a sack of potatoes.

*Please, Lord Jesus, protect us! Guide us to safety!*

"Keep your head down!" Marsh barked. The car's swaying intensified before it seemed to straighten out somewhat. Had they reached a road? She didn't dare lift her head to find out.

For long moments there was nothing but silence. She wanted to believe the lack of gunfire was reassuring, but for all she knew, the car behind them was focused on closing the gap between them.

After another long five minutes, Marsh broke the silence. "Okay, you can sit up now. We've lost him."

Cautiously, she lifted her head. They had crossed a farmer's field but now appeared to be on a dirt road. To the right she caught a glimpse of an abandoned farmhouse. Twisting in her seat, she looked behind them for headlights, trying to relax when she didn't see any. "Are you sure?"

"Yeah." Marsh's expression was grim, but the corner of his mouth quirked in a crooked smile. "While trying to follow us across the field, he hit a rock and blew out a tire."

"We're safe," she whispered with gratitude.

"For now." Marsh scowled. "I don't like how that man tailed us from your neighborhood. After running from your place, the knife guy must have hidden nearby waiting for us to drive past. This is my fault. I should have asked the locals to search the entire area for him."

The idea of the knife-wielding man waiting for her so he could finish the job filled her with fear and dread. "He's not going to stop until he has the code."

"Hey, don't worry." Marsh reached for her hand. "I'll keep you safe."

She trusted Marsh the same way she trusted her brother Tucker or the other rangers he worked with. She hadn't interacted much with Jackson Woodlow or Sam Hayward, but knew they were good men.

Decent. Kind. Willing to put their lives on the line for others.

"Thank you." Her voice thickened with tears and she tried to blink them away. Pregnancy hormones didn't help, but nearly being killed for the second time in a matter of hours had badly shaken her. She drew in a deep, steadying breath and asked, "What's the plan?"

"Find a place to stay," Marsh responded without hesitation. He turned right onto another highway. They were in a part of the outskirts of San Antonio that she'd never seen before.

"I thought we were going to your place?"

"That's no longer an option. Not when that guy may have taken note of my license plate number. Unfortunately, it's too late to get a rental car, tonight." He released her hand to rub his chin. "We'll have to improvise until tomorrow morning."

She wasn't sure what that meant but trusted Marsh's ability to evade her attacker. Irrationally, she was angry with Dan for stealing the code in the first place, getting himself killed and putting her and their unborn daughter in danger.

What husband did that?

She'd thought Dan was sweet and kind. He'd seemed to truly care about her. But those last few weeks before his murder, she knew something was wrong. She'd tried to get him to open up and talk to her, but he kept insisting he was fine. That things were good.

Another lie, she thought wearily. It was only after his death that she'd learned he'd been fired from his job at the tech company.

Had he been let go because of the mysterious code? Or had he stolen it after being fired to make extra money? Or was the code from something else?

With a concerted effort, she forced the useless thoughts aside. No point in wishing things were different. That Dan had been a better man. A better husband. Still alive to put an end to this issue with the missing code. Looking back was useless. She needed to look forward. To stay focused on figuring out where Dan would have hidden a stolen code.

His computer was the most logical place to keep important information, but the police had mentioned that had been taken by the guy who'd killed him outside the ATM machine. They had the robbery on tape—a masked man shot and killed Dan, then snatched his computer and phone. Knowing about the missing code and Dan's role in stealing it brought a greater significance to the theft of the device.

Good thing she still had her laptop. Could she access Dan's computer programs? Some of them maybe. His email for sure, but she didn't think he'd be so foolish as to email the code to himself. Besides if it was that easy to find, the knife guy would already have it.

Wouldn't he?

"Are you okay?" Marsh asked. "You're awfully quiet."

"Fine." She smoothed her hands over her belly. The baby was quiet, too; she generally moved around the most when Stacy was trying to sleep. "The night Dan was murdered, his computer was taken along with his phone. We know now the real reason he was killed was to find the code."

Marsh shrugged. "If they wanted the code, why kill him? That's not logical. They'd find a way to force him into giving them the information."

"True." She swallowed hard as her thoughts whirled. "Unless Dan gave them a fake code. But before they could test it to see if it worked, something happened, forcing them to kill him. They took his laptop, figuring they'd find what they needed, but when that didn't work, they came after me."

"Almost three months later?" Marsh's tone was skeptical. "I'd have expected them to come sooner."

"Maybe they couldn't. Maybe they had to break into his computer and search all his files before they realized the code was still missing." She threw up her hands. "I don't know why they came after me now. Especially when I don't have any idea what Dan was doing. What he'd gotten involved in."

"I understand, Stacy. I'm not blaming you." His low husky voice was a balm to her nerves. "We're brainstorming theories, that's all."

She told herself to remain calm. Getting upset wasn't helping. As a Texas Ranger, Marsh had resources he could tap into. Maybe he could figure out where Dan hid the code. Or what he was doing prior to his death.

Then she abruptly straightened. They both worked in the tech industry. Dan was well versed in computer programing; it was his area of expertise. But she worked in the tech field, too.

Her husband wouldn't have hidden his stolen code in her computer programs.

Would he?

An icy chill snaked down her spine. She didn't want to believe Dan had purposefully put her in danger. But after uncovering his lies and this latest missing and stolen code, she understood anything was possible.

Navigating the back roads toward Austin took longer than Marsh liked, but it couldn't be helped. He needed to avoid the interstate, especially since he had no idea who they were dealing with.

A low-level crook? His gut was telling him that wasn't the case. And that while only one man had broken into Stacy's home, a stolen code gave him the impression that more assailants were likely involved.

He hated knowing she was in danger and silently

vowed to keep her safe no matter what. He cared about her, and as Tucker's friend, he knew his fellow ranger would expect him to do everything possible to protect her.

When Stacy shifted in her seat for the third time in as many minutes, he frowned with concern. "What's wrong?"

She avoided his gaze. "I need to use the bathroom."

He gave himself a mental head slap. He should have anticipated her needs. "No problem. We'll find a place to stop." They were approaching the town of Seguin and while it was too close to the area where they'd lost the car following them, it would work for a few minutes.

He slowed and made his way through the town known for its amusement park. Tourists flocked to the area during the winter months when their mild weather was nothing compared to the snow and cold up north.

Spying a gas station/convenience store, he turned into the parking lot. The look of relief in Stacy's eyes made him realize she'd needed to stop for a while. He wasn't used to traveling with a pregnant woman.

She pushed out of the car before he could get around to help her. Lengthening his stride, he caught up and rested his hand on her back as they walked inside.

"Would you like something to eat?" He gestured to the rows of snacks. "I'm not sure how long we'll be on the road."

"Water and maybe some high-protein granola bars." She flashed a weary smile. She didn't linger but headed straight for the restrooms.

Marsh bought several bags of snacks, including her requested protein bars and a can of stacked chips that he knew she liked. After adding two bottles of water, he paid for the items.

He grew concerned when Stacy didn't return right away. Imagining her breaking down in there had him crossing to the door. "Stacy? Are you okay?"

"Just a minute." Her voice was muffled and he could tell she had been crying. Feeling helpless, he stood there waiting. He was so close he could hear her blowing her nose and washing her hands.

When the door finally opened, she didn't meet his gaze. Her eyes were red and puffy. "I'm fine."

She wasn't and they both knew it. "What can I do?" he asked, taking her hand in his. "How can I help you feel better?"

A spark of annoyance lit her blue eyes. "You can't control my feelings, Marsh." Then she sighed and added, "I can't seem to control them, either. I was okay until I saw the scratch along my neck…" Her voice trailed off. "I'd never been so scared in my life as when he held that knife at my throat. I was worried I would die and so would my baby."

"I wish I could have been there for you." If her idiot husband was still alive, he'd punch him in the gut for putting Stacy in this position.

"I'm fine," she repeated with a little more conviction. "Let's go."

"I need to top off my gas tank." He had burned through fuel in his haste to reach her side and to escape the guy shooting at them. "It will only take a few minutes."

She nodded without saying anything, wiping at her swollen eyes, and it was all he could do not to pull her into his arms. Reminding himself that she was Tucker's little sister and pregnant and grieving her jerk of a husband was more than enough to keep him from acting on his impulse.

Besides, Stacy deserved someone who would be there for her. His previous girlfriend, Annette, had flat out told him his career wasn't conducive to relationships, shifting the blame for her failures onto his shoulders. And deep down, he'd known she was right. Even now, two years later, he watched his close friends, Tucker and Sam, as they did their best to balance career and family. And as much as they were both now happily married, he'd noticed how much they missed their respective spouses while they were out working a case.

Shaking off the depressing thoughts about his lonely future, he escorted Stacy to the SUV and held the door open for her. Then he quickly used his credit card to fill the tank. He swept his gaze over the area but didn't expect the gunman to show.

The hour was going on midnight. Based on Stacy's exhaustion and emotional fragility, his initial plan to drive straight through to Austin wasn't feasible.

There was a town called Lockton that wasn't too far away. It was halfway between their current location and Austin, and well off the main route. When he finished filling the tank, he settled behind the wheel.

Stacy sat with her eyes closed, her palms resting on her belly. He hesitated, unsure if she was sleeping.

"I can feel you staring at me." She turned her head to look at him.

"Sorry." He started the engine. "We'll find a place in Lockton, okay? That's about thirty-three miles from here."

"Whatever you think is best." She sounded sad but then abruptly straightened. "Oh, that was a strong one."

"What?" He shot her a look of panic. "Not a contraction? It's too early!"

"No, not a contraction," she said. "She kicked me."

"She?" The panic didn't subside. If anything, her comment only reinforced his lack of experience with this kind of thing. "You know the baby is a girl?"

"Yes, I'm having a girl, at least according to the ultrasound." She rubbed her belly. "One who apparently intends to play soccer."

He couldn't help but grin, despite his fears. "Maybe she'll be a martial arts expert."

"Anything she wants to do is fine with me." Stacy's smile faded. "I'm trying not to think the worst, but I still can't believe Dan did this to me. That he lied about losing his job and put me in danger over this stupid code."

"Wait, what do you mean he lied about losing his job?" That was news to him. "When did you find out?"

"About two weeks after his death." She grimaced. "I was waiting for his last paycheck to be deposited in our joint account. When it didn't show up, I called Tech Guard, the computer company he worked for. They said he'd been let go a month earlier."

He couldn't imagine why Dan would have kept that a secret. "I don't understand. Didn't you notice he hadn't been getting regular payroll deposits?"

"That's just it. There were deposits." She glanced at him. "I assumed they gave him some sort of severance. Maybe paying him through that last month prior to cutting him off for good."

"If so, then it doesn't sound like he was fired for

cause," Marsh said. "Employees don't get severance pack-ages even for a short time frame like a month if they're fired for misconduct, stealing or whatever."

"I have no idea why he was let go," she admitted. "The human resources woman I spoke to wouldn't give me any information. Other than providing his last date of employ-ment. At the time it didn't seem to matter. Now I'm not so sure what he was doing when I was working."

"Hmm." The mystery around her deceased husband and the infamous stolen code was getting deeper by the minute. "What exactly was Dan's area of expertise?"

"He was an information technology security program-ing expert." When Marsh raised a brow, she added, "You know, reinforcing firewalls against cybersecurity attacks. Preventing malware from infecting a company's entire system. That kind of thing."

"Not exactly my area of expertise," he said with a shrug. "Sounds important."

"Yeah, it is." She fell silent again for a long moment. "It would make sense that the code is related to computer codes, but I'm not sure how a code like that could be sto-len. Or even why? That part really doesn't make sense."

"Corporate espionage?" he asked.

"You mean Dan stole the code from a competitor?" She frowned. "I guess that's possible. But that type of code would be a huge file downloaded on a USB drive or some other type of portable hard drive. It's not like a ten- or twelve-digit code to a lockbox or bank account or anything like that. Besides, why would the competition kill him for that? Why not have him arrested?"

"We're going to need an IT specialist to figure this out," he muttered half to himself.

"I work with computer technology, too. My area isn't security like Dan's. I build software programs. That's how we met." There was a slight hitch in her tone as she added, "At a computer technology conference in Houston."

"I see." Although he really didn't. Building software sounded very different from cybersecurity. "I didn't realize you met at a conference."

"Yes. We had so much in common. Or so I thought. He told me he was an only child and that his parents had died when he was in college. And that was the reason he wanted to have a large family." She smoothed her hand over her belly. "Now here I am, alone and in trouble over his actions." She slowly shook her head. "I never expected him to do something like this."

Marsh knew a little about that. "It's hard when your trust gets broken like that. My former girlfriend was cheating on me with her old high school boyfriend. I don't just mean a quick meetup here and there, but more like she was living two completely separate lives. One with me and one with Brad." He glanced at her, then turned his attention back to the road. "As you know from Tuck, our job requires a fair amount of travel. My erratic schedule made it easy for Annette to split her time between the two of us. And when I finally figured it out and confronted her, she acted like it was no big deal. As if I should be happy she had someone to spend time with while I was gone. She basically blamed my job for her indiscretion."

"That's awful," Stacy said with a frown. "Nobody would think that's okay."

"She found that out the hard way. Turns out Brad wasn't too thrilled with her double life, either." He managed a wry grin. "He kicked her to the curb. I guess her dual lives finally caught up with her." Normally he wouldn't share so much about his private life, but considering everything she'd been through, he wanted her to know she wasn't alone.

"I'm starting to think Dan had two different lives, too," she said. "The sweet, kind, caring husband he pretended to be while also working behind my back with criminals."

He grimaced. "I know it's difficult to comprehend something like this. And your situation is worse. At least all I lost was a woman who wasn't who I thought she was."

"I lost a man who wasn't who I thought he was, too." She waved a hand. "But that's on them, right? Not us."

"Right." He tried to smile, but it wasn't easy. After a few minutes of silence, he asked, "So back to this computer stuff that you and your late husband did for a living. Do you have some idea where to start searching for the code?"

"Sort of." She sighed again. "It's a good thing I brought my laptop and that I had it in my car rather than in the office when the knife guy showed up. I'd originally grabbed it so that I could get some work done. But obviously things have changed. I have a bad feeling Dan hid the stolen code in plain sight. Not within any of his computer programs but in mine."

Her programs? A flash of anger hit hard. How could Dan have done something like that? "He had to know that stealing a code and hiding in on your computer programs would place you and your baby in danger."

"Yeah, well, apparently he didn't care." Bitterness laced her tone.

Marsh couldn't blame her for being upset. First, she had lost her husband to a violent crime, then learned he'd lied to her about his job and who knew what else, and now this. Her husband's betrayal had placed her squarely in the killer's crosshairs.

The way Dan had callously placed his wife and unborn child in danger was unconscionable. Granted Dan couldn't have known he'd be murdered, maybe he assumed he'd be around to protect Stacy and the baby.

Marsh steeled his resolve to protect them with his life. No matter what.

His phone rang, interrupting his thoughts. Seeing Tucker's name on the screen, he used the hands-free function to answer. "Hey, Tuck, I'm with Stacy. Everything is fine."

"I'm glad to hear Stacy is with you, but things are not fine. Leanne called to let me know two guys showed up at the Rocking T looking for Stacy. They claimed to be with the federal government but took off when she pressed to inspect their IDs more closely. She didn't like the way they'd flashed their creds without giving her a chance to see them."

The news shocked him. "That's not good."

"Nope. I don't know if they're really feds or just a couple of bad actors, but I'm relocating Pops and Leanne off the ranch until further notice. Stick close to Stacy. We'll reconnect in the morning to figure out what's going on."

"I will." He hit the End Call button.

"Feds," Stacy whispered. "What's that about?"

He had no clue. The information added a new dimension to the case.

Making him wonder who they could trust.

# THREE

By the time they reached Lockton, Stacy was so tired she could barely see straight. Her mind spun, reliving the events over and over until she wanted to scream.

Yet her body craved rest. Once they were settled in their ground-level one-bedroom suite—the only option Marsh would consider upon learning the hotel didn't have connecting rooms—she'd opened her laptop and logged in to her email. But the words swam on the screen, making her realize it was no use. She wouldn't be able to think clearly without sleep.

"Stacy?" Marsh's low husky voice from across the room sent shivers down her spine. Inappropriate shivers and she blamed her pregnancy hormones for this weird awareness of Marshall Branson.

Dan had only been gone three months. What kind of grieving widow was she, anyway?

"What?" She hadn't meant to sound crabby. "Sorry. I'm tired."

"I was hoping to borrow your computer." He gestured to the device. "I'll do some digging while you rest."

"Go ahead." She waved a hand at the laptop. "Although you should get some sleep, too."

"I will." Marsh moved over to the table as she stepped back. "Rest well. I'm here."

Her crabbiness melted. "I know. Thanks." When he dropped into the chair she'd vacated, she turned to head into the bedroom Marsh had insisted she take. After washing up, she crawled into bed.

The next thing she knew, sunlight streamed in through the window. One thing about being pregnant, the baby kicking her bladder worked better than an alarm clock.

Her stomach rumbled with hunger. After a quick shower and donning fresh clothes, she took a moment to rummage in her suitcase for her bottle of prenatal vitamins. Then followed the enticing scent of coffee.

Opening the door to the suite, she poked her head through to make sure he was decent. "Marsh? Are you awake?"

"Yes." He stood beside the sofa where he must have slept, a grin creasing his handsome features. "Wow, you look great. Are you hungry? I'll order breakfast."

For a moment this little interlude seemed like a vacation. Marsh was acting sweet, as if they had nothing more important to worry about than sharing a meal. But as she spied the open laptop Marsh had set on the coffee table, the events from the previous night washed over her.

"Did you find anything useful?" She dropped onto the sofa, setting her bottle of vitamins on the table next to the computer. "Something to help us figure out who the knife guy is?"

"I found something interesting, but it's not going to be much help," Marsh said. He slid the room service menu toward her. "Pick what you'd like. We should eat first."

That sounded ominous, but she went ahead and

scanned the menu. "I'll have the breakfast burrito with juice and decaf coffee." Giving up caffeine had not been easy, but she had also grown accustomed to drinking herbal tea. "Thanks."

"Sounds good." He picked up the phone and placed their order.

She waited until he'd finished. "Please tell me what you found."

He sighed and sat on the sofa beside her. He reached out to take her hands and cradled them in his. The gentleness of his fingers warmed her heart. "It's more a matter of what I didn't find. Which is why the information isn't much help."

"I don't understand." She frowned. "What does that mean?"

"Let's go back in time for a few minutes," he suggested. "You mentioned meeting your husband at the conference in Houston. That was, what, a little over two years ago?"

"That's correct. We dated for a few months, got engaged, then married." She frowned. "I know Tuck ran Dan's criminal record since he always did that with the guys I dated, and I know that he didn't find anything. Dan was clean, which is why I was so shocked to hear that he stole a code."

"Did Dan mention his personal life?" Marsh asked. "Where he grew up? Where his family is from?"

She waved her hand impatiently. "Yes, of course we talked about our families. I told you a little of that already. He grew up in the Midwest, went to college at Iowa State and got a degree in computer science. His parents died while he was a sophomore at Iowa."

"No extended family?" Marsh pressed.

She shot him an exasperated glance, not sure where he was going with this. "Dan mentioned he didn't invite his two cousins on his dad's side of the family to our wedding because there was some sort of feud that split the family apart. He probably has other extended family, but I've never met them." She dropped her gaze to her hands. "I didn't have a large funeral for him anyway, because I couldn't afford it. Not that I would have known how to contact his cousins."

"You put an obituary in the newspaper, right?" he asked.

"Yes, of course." She shrugged. "But I wasn't surprised when nobody reached out. Especially considering Dan said he and his cousins weren't close."

Marsh looked thoughtful. "So, other than where he went to college and meeting him at the conference, you don't know much about him."

"I know he worked for Tech Guard for five years, relocating here to San Antonio after he finished college. That's partially why hearing he lost his job was so surprising. It's not like he was a brand-new employee who might mess something up." She scowled. "What's going on, Marsh? Why are the details of Dan's background so important?"

He was silent for a long time, and she found herself holding her breath, dreading what he might reveal. Then he finally said, "I used our state criminal investigative computer system to do a deep dive on your husband, Daniel Copeland. I've been in touch with our IT expert, Nina, early this morning and she confirmed my suspicions. Dan Copeland doesn't exist. His driver's license goes back to the point when he was eighteen. Nothing earlier. No jobs prior to that, and the Social Security number he was using isn't real. It's fake. Furthermore, if he attended college, it wasn't under the name of Dan Copeland."

An icy chill ran down her spine. A fake Social Security number? Not attending college? "That's not possible. There must be some mistake. Dan would have needed a four-year degree to get his job at Tech Guard." Even as she said the words, she realized that maybe his falsifying his college education was the reason he'd been let go. "They'd have checked into his background prior to hiring him, wouldn't they?"

"Maybe they only did a cursory look. He may have been savvy enough to have created a diploma showing he graduated. If he seemed to know his stuff, I'm sure they wouldn't have looked twice."

"He mentioned his friend Matt Wade helped him get the job."

"Matt Wade?" Marsh's voice filled with anticipation. "That's good to know. We can see if he's involved in some way." Marsh hesitated, then said, "Do you know for sure Dan was employed at Tech Guard for five years? What if it was less?"

Marsh had a point. If Dan had lied about being fired, maybe he hadn't worked there for as long as he'd claimed. "That should be easy enough to validate through tracking his fake Social Security number, right?" she replied.

"I'll work on that," Marsh agreed.

She still couldn't believe they were having this conversation. Her throat went dry, and she had to swallow hard before speaking. "If my husband's name wasn't really Dan Copeland, then who was he? And why would he lie about his life?"

"Those are good questions. Answers we need to uncover sooner rather than later." Marsh held her gaze. "I have a bad feeling about this, Stacy. I don't know if those guys who headed to the ranch were really feds or not, but if they are employed by the government, then I'd have to assume they're from homeland security."

She blanched. "You don't seriously think Dan was some sort of terrorist?"

"I don't know what he was." After a brief hesitation, he added, "But it's looking as if that stolen code is a bigger deal than we realized."

"A bigger deal, how?" She frowned, trying to follow his logic, but her thoughts were bouncing around wildly as she struggled to absorb what she had just learned—that the man she'd married wasn't who she thought he was at all. "Domestic terrorism of some sort? That's impossible. Dan didn't have any secret meetings or anything like that." She wondered if they were letting their imagination run wild. The man she'd known was nice, somewhat nerdy and not at all what she imagined a terrorist would be. Okay, so he faked…some things. That didn't mean he would do worse, right? Even as she asked herself the question, she recoiled at the possible answer. She hadn't known Dan, or whoever he was, at all.

As if reading her mind, Marsh shook his head. "Don't sell him short. The man you married changed his name at the age of eighteen and obtained a fake Social Security number for a reason. Your late husband could have hacked into the government's IT systems, maybe into classified documents of some sort. Maybe they didn't even realize it until now."

"Talk about a conspiracy theory." She worked hard not to reveal her inner panic. What he was describing was surreal. "You're grasping at straws."

"Maybe. Let's just disregard the various possibilities and focus on the facts," he agreed. "I still think it's strange that there's no record of Dan Copeland graduating college. And nothing prior to his first driver's license hitting the system at age eighteen. No birth certificate on file, either. It's almost as if he materialized out of thin air. He had some other jobs that were also in the IT world, so he must have gotten an education from somewhere. I have Nina digging for information from those companies to make sure that the Dan Copeland who worked there is the same guy you married."

And if he wasn't? Could her husband have stolen more than the code? Like some other man's identity? She stared at Marsh in stunned silence.

Was it possible for a man to create a new identify for himself as Marsh suggested? Or worse, take over some other man's life?

She'd thought learning about Dan's lie about losing his job was bad, but this? Hearing her husband was a man with no past was far worse.

Who was Dan Copeland? And what in the world had he gotten her involved in?

Watching the myriad emotions playing across Stacy's face was heart-wrenching. Marsh felt bad about having to be the one to tell her the man she'd loved didn't exist.

One possibility was that her husband had been in Witness Protection. But if that was the case, there would be a better paper trail. The US Marshals Service didn't leave loose ends. They'd have created an entire background for their protectee, one that would not raise suspicions.

No, the more he thought about the guy holding Stacy at knifepoint and then shooting at them from a moving car, the more he believed Dan had changed his name and gotten a fake Social Security number to cover his tracks. Because he'd done something bad and needed to disappear.

A plan that hadn't worked, as someone must have figured out the truth. And maybe that's the reason he'd been shot and killed near the ATM machine.

"This is too much for me to comprehend," she whispered. "How could Dan have created a new identity?"

"There are ways," Marsh said. "You had Dan's body cremated, didn't you?" He remembered Tucker saying something about that but hadn't paid much attention.

She nodded slowly. "Yes. I understand what you're asking. If he had been embalmed, we could run his DNA to see if there's a match in the system. I—if I had known..."

"There's no way you could have, so don't beat yourself up over that. We can try lifting some fingerprints from your house." The trashed office flashed in his memory, making that a less viable option. "Maybe your master suite?"

"I clean every couple of weeks." She rested her hand on her belly. "I gave his clothes away, too, and the couple of items I kept have all been laundered." She shook her head. "I can't think of any place where you could get his DNA or fingerprints."

"You sold his car?" Marsh wished now that he'd have

done a deeper dive into her husband before now. Tucker would kick himself sideways, too.

"Yes. To help pay bills." She abruptly lifted her head, her blue eyes gleaming with excitement. "Wait a minute. There's an insurance card in my glove box. Dan put it there after paying the bill. I haven't touched it since, as I've had no reason to. Would that work?"

"Absolutely we can give that a try." He smiled reassuringly. "Good thinking on your part." DNA would have been better, but he'd take what he could get. A fingerprint might reveal Dan Copeland's real identity, if he was running from a criminal past as Marsh suspected.

If not? He inwardly winced. No sense imagining the worst-case scenario.

He stood and reached for his phone to call Jackson. "I need a favor."

"Okay, what's going on?" Jackson asked.

Marsh quickly filled his fellow ranger in on the danger Stacy was in and what he'd learned about a deep dive into Dan Copeland's background. "I need you to get to Stacy's home in San Antonio to get the insurance card from her glove box. Have it tested for prints and see what name pops in the system. We need to understand what we're up against here."

"I can do that," Jackson agreed. "Where's Tuck?"

"Moving his wife Leanne and Pops to a new location." He frowned, remembering how Stacy had taught him how to perform ranch chores during their time together. "Not sure who's caring for the livestock while they're gone."

"Tuck will have found someone to lend a hand," Jackson said. "I would offer to chip in to help, but I have never actually worked on a ranch."

He had, learning the ropes from Stacy herself. "I can do it." Marsh felt obligated to take on the chore. He didn't like the idea of leaving Stacy's side, but she should be safe enough with her brother. "I'll touch base with Tucker soon. I can always drop Stacy wherever he's staying with Pops and Leanne, then head down to the Rocking T."

"Whatever works," Jackson said. "I'll get that insurance card. Sounds like getting those prints processed will be the best way to break open the case."

"Call me as soon as you know something." He ended the call as someone knocked at the door.

"Room service," a female voice called out.

"Get back, Stacy." He gestured for her to move back inside the bedroom. She looked exasperated but didn't argue. When she was safely out of the way, he crossed to the door to peer out into the hallway. A woman stood there holding a tray with two covered plates, a carafe of decaf coffee and a glass of juice. After a long second, Marsh stepped back and opened the door.

"Thanks." He took the tray, set it on the table and then reached into his pocket for a tip. The female server glanced around curiously but didn't make any threatening moves.

"Thank you, sir," she said, accepting the tip. After she left, Marsh felt foolish for being so paranoid. It was his nature to be cautious, but he was confident they hadn't been followed.

And it was a man who'd held Stacy at gunpoint. Not a woman.

"Marsh? Is everything okay?" Stacy poked her head through the doorway.

"Yes. Our food is here." He stepped to the side, giving her room to head to the small table. The suite should have been plenty large, but it seemed small and cramped.

Or maybe it just felt that way because he was so keenly aware of Stacy. Ridiculous for him to be attracted to his best friend's pregnant sister.

Maybe he needed his head examined.

"I'd like to say grace," Stacy said, interrupting his self-incriminating thoughts.

"Of course." He knew Stacy and Tucker had found their faith the same way Sam Hayward and his wife Mari had. He sat beside her and bowed his head.

"Dear Lord Jesus, we ask You to bless this food we are about to eat. We also ask that You please guide us to safety. Amen."

"Amen," Marsh echoed. He looked at Stacy, who was staring down at her abdomen. "Hey, try not to worry. We're going to catch up to Tucker, Leanne and Pops very soon."

"What?" She lifted her head. "No. I don't want to put them in danger."

He frowned. "Stacy, you must know Tucker and Leanne are more than capable of keeping you safe." Tucker was a Texas Ranger, and his wife Leanne worked as the Chief Deputy for the small Diamond County Sheriff's Department. Two cops could protect Stacy and her grandfather.

"Leanne is pregnant," Stacy said, a stubborn glint in her eye. "She's not far along, only ten weeks, so they weren't saying much publicly yet, but I won't put her in danger."

That news was a surprise, but Marsh knew Tucker and Leanne were still more than capable of protecting them-

selves. Stacy turned and reached for her bottle of vitamins. She dropped what looked like a horse pill into her
palm and took a sip of her orange juice to wash it down.

They ate in silence for several minutes. Preoccupied
with the tasks before him, Marsh tried not to feel de-
pressed about handing Stacy over to her brother.

Despite her fears over Leanne's early pregnancy, he
knew Tucker would rather have Stacy with them. Even
if Tucker didn't need him to watch over the ranch, handing Stacy off would give Marsh the freedom to do the
legwork on the case.

"I need to call my boss to let him know I won't be in
for work," Stacy said, breaking the silence. "I should have
thought of that earlier. I don't like using my sick time. I
was saving it for my maternity leave."

He nodded. "I understand, but your safety is more
important right now." Then he remembered how she'd
worked from the ranch. "Once we get you with Tucker
and Leanne, you can probably work remotely."

"I told you, I don't want to put Leanne or Pops in danger." She shot him an exasperated look. "Yes, I can work
remotely, but we can do that from here, right? Or would
you rather head all the way to Austin?"

He sighed. She was more stubborn than Tucker, and
that was saying something. "We are not staying here
in Lockton. Our next location depends on where your
brother ends up with his wife and your grandfather. I'm
sure he'll want to be in a larger city where they can get
lost in the shuffle."

She narrowed her gaze. Pursing her lips with annoyance, she finished her breakfast burrito, grabbed her bottle of vitamins from the table and rose to her feet. She

then picked up her computer. "I'll pack my things, as it's clear you want to hit the road. But I'll talk to my brother, too." She jutted her chin, eyeing him narrowly. "I'm sure I can convince him that we should stay miles apart. That you dropping me off by him will only put everyone in danger. It's not like Pops can move fast if things go bad."

"Go ahead and talk to him." Marsh was confident Tuck would be on his side, despite Leanne's pregnancy and his grandfather's older age. Pops might have some physical limitations, but Marsh knew from personal experience that the older man could wield a rifle and a shotgun. Much like Stacy's neighbor, Hank, Pops could hold his own if needed.

Marsh quickly finished his meal, then stood to stack the dishes. He didn't have anything to pack, so once Stacy was ready, they'd hit the road.

As he opened the door to set the tray outside, a flash of movement caught his eye. Reacting on pure gut instinct, he slammed the door shut, flipped the lock and threw himself to the side as gunfire erupted. Six bullets penetrated the wood.

They'd been found!

# FOUR

Gunfire! Heart lodged in her throat, Stacy grabbed her computer case and slung it over her shoulder before darting into the bathroom and closing the door behind her.

Not that the door or even her laptop would prevent a bullet from killing her and her baby. Frantic, she pulled the edges of her coat tighter around her torso, positioning the laptop in front of her belly as if that would help. Then she eyed the ceramic bathtub, deciding it may also provide some protection. Although once she got down inside, it wouldn't be easy to get back out. Still, she threw one leg over the side of the tub when she heard Marsh's voice.

"Stacy!"

"In here." Abandoning her plan, she moved toward the bathroom door just as it opened.

Marsh stood, weapon in hand, his expression grim. "We need to move."

"Where?" She hurried to his side, grateful when he put his arm around her shoulders.

He ushered her toward the bedroom window that faced the back of the hotel. Releasing her, he raised the sash, used his fist to punch through screen and then turned to her. "Climb out. Hurry." They were on the first floor, and the sill was low enough that she wouldn't have to jump.

If she'd thought getting in and out of the tub was difficult, this was worse. Especially with the laptop case. But she didn't complain, leaning heavily on Marsh for support. She'd just cleared the window when she heard more gunfire.

*Not Marsh! Please Lord, not Marsh!*

As if in answer to her prayers, Marsh shimmied through the window to stand beside her. His somber expression gave her the impression he'd been the source of the gunfire. "Let's go."

She nodded, her throat tight with fear. Marsh took her hand in his, keeping the weapon in his other hand as he led her across the back side of the hotel. Up ahead, she could see another commercial property of some sort.

A restaurant?

The breakfast burrito she'd eaten churned in her belly. She swallowed hard as Marsh set a brisk pace. Not running, as that would be difficult for her, but a fast walk. The computer bag bumped against her side. Ignoring the discomfort, she did her best to keep up as he led her through the parking lot of the restaurant, then down the road.

As they walked, Marsh swept his gaze from side to side, clearly searching for signs of a threat. She tried to do the same, although she wasn't sure if she'd recognize the bad guys if she saw them. The knife-wielding man maybe, but anyone else? Doubtful.

And how had they been found at the hotel in Lockton?

"This way." Marsh abruptly turned down another side street. Her heart still pounded with fear and exertion, but as the balmy air washed over her, she was grateful to be wearing a sweater. And that she'd managed to hang on to the laptop.

She wished there'd been time to grab her suitcase. But the only thing she really needed was her prenatal vitamins. And they could be replaced. Marsh took another turn, and moments later they arrived at the Corner Coffee Café. As if on cue, the wail of sirens could be heard.

The police responding to the scene of the crime.

"I need to call Jackson." Marsh subtly slipped his gun into his holster while leading her to a small table tucked in the corner of the room. "I'll buy something for us to drink. Decaf, right?" At her nod, he added, "Better to be paying customers if we need to hang out here for a while."

Sinking gratefully into the chair, she removed the computer case and rested the bag on the floor. She glanced around the half-full café. Thankfully, no one seemed to be paying any attention to her; most were on their phones or laptop computers. "Do you think it's safe?"

"For now." His cryptic comment didn't invite more questions. Remembering the gunfire and his grim expression after they'd escaped through the window, she assumed he may have shot and killed the gunman.

Marsh took his place in line, smiled at the barista and placed their order. Then, while waiting for the coffee, he used his phone to call Jackson. From her spot at the table, she couldn't hear what he was saying. Their discussion didn't take long, and within two minutes Marsh had their drinks in hand and was making his way back to the table.

"Thank you." She wrapped her hands around the coffee cup, savoring the warmth. "What did Jackson say?"

"He's on his way." Marsh barely sipped his coffee, his

dark eyes darting from the window looking at the street, to the customers moving around the café. "He'll help secure a rental car."

It took a moment for her to understand. "You think they tracked us to the hotel via your car?"

He shrugged and finally met her gaze. "That's the most logical answer. The gunman who followed us from your house must have gotten the license plate."

"So, why wait until morning to make the attempt against us?"

He grimaced. "They knew we were at the hotel, but not in which room we were staying. The woman who delivered our food must have been paid to provide information. It was a man who I saw lingering in the hallway."

She was afraid to ask what happened to him. But Marsh must have read the unspoken question in her gaze.

"I fired at him to buy us time to get away. He went down, so I know I hit him, but I don't know if he's alive or dead."

Again, her stomach knotted. "I'm sorry you were in that position."

He held her gaze for a long moment. "I only did what was necessary to keep you safe. Besides, it's my fault. The way that woman looked around with interest should have tipped me off that she was up to no good."

"It's not your fault. It's Dan's." She leaned forward to touch Marsh's hand. "And there's no way you could have known the room service lady was involved."

He looked away and pulled his hand from her touch. He sipped his coffee, once again staring out the window. The wailing sirens had quieted as they reached their destination. She could easily imagine the police officers scouring the hotel, searching for them as the occupants of the room.

"The police will eventually find our fingerprints in the hotel room." She pushed her decaf coffee away. It was making her feel sick. "I don't think mine are in the system, but I assume yours are. They'll know we were there."

"Yeah." Marsh seemed to have already considered that possibility. "But we'll be long gone by then. I'm more interested in whether they'll find the gunman there."

"You don't want to talk to them—the police?" she asked.

He sighed. "Not yet. Not until I know more."

She shivered, imagining the horrible man who'd held her at knifepoint lying dead in the room. She felt bad Marsh had been forced to shoot the guy.

If the bad guy was dead or injured badly enough to need the hospital, did that mean the danger was over?

Somehow, she doubted it. Even though the bad guy had claimed Dan had stolen the code, she didn't think he was working alone.

And based on how Marsh remained on high alert, she understood he didn't think so, either.

Marsh tried not to stare at his watch as they waited for Jackson to arrive. His fellow ranger was doing everything he could to get there. It wasn't Jackson's fault he was driving in from Austin.

The good news was that Jackson had retrieved the insurance card from Stacy's vehicle last night. Jackson had taken the card to the state crime lab to be processed, rather than leaving that task to the local police.

They'd learned their lesson the hard way months ago

when some dirty cops had tried to kill Tucker and Leanne. No more trusting the locals. Oh, he knew that dirty cops were rare and that it wasn't fair to paint them all with the same brush, but he wasn't taking any chances when it came to keeping Stacy alive.

Jackson had wholeheartedly agreed.

Marsh finished his coffee and debated getting another. He didn't need more caffeine zipping through his system. He was ready to jump out of his skin being forced to sit there, basically hiding in plain sight. But Stacy was pregnant, which meant that dragging her down one street after another to reach the other side of the city wasn't an option.

When Stacy rose to her feet, he shot up from his chair. "Where are you going?"

"The bathroom." Her cheeks flushed and she looked away. "Frequent visits are part of being pregnant."

"I'll go with you." When her eyes widened in horror, he quickly added, "I'll make use of the facilities, too."

She relaxed and reached for the computer case. He quickly snagged it. As she headed toward the bathrooms, he stayed right behind her.

When he was finished, he waited for her, hoping she wouldn't break down crying like she had at the gas station last night. Not that he could blame her.

He'd promised to keep her safe, and so far, he was doing a lousy job of it. The near miss at the hotel was sobering.

If he'd been a few seconds later, they'd both be dead. And things had happened so fast, he couldn't even be sure if the shooter matched the description Stacy had provided. White, with darker skin, possibly mixed race.

A firm image of the gunman wouldn't gel in his mind.

He was still trying to come up with at least one identifying feature when Stacy emerged from the restroom, stopping short when she saw him standing there. "Are we staying? Or going?"

On cue, his phone buzzed. Pulling it from his pocket, he was relieved to see Jackson's name on the screen. "I'll tell you in a sec." He lifted the phone to his ear. "Hey, Jackson. Where are you?"

"Outside the coffee shop."

"We'll be right out." He pocketed his phone and reached for Stacy's hand. "Jackson's here."

"Great." Her blue eyes flared with relief.

Battling guilt, Marsh escorted her through the coffee shop to the main entrance. Jackson was waiting right outside the front door, having parked the SUV in a delivery zone. Marsh pushed open the door and glanced both ways before stepping outside. He held the door for Stacy, who gratefully hurried toward the SUV. Marsh stayed behind her, waiting for her to slide in behind Jackson, then storing the computer bag on the floor beside her.

He rounded the back of the vehicle to climb in beside his fellow ranger. The minute he was seated, Jackson put the SUV in Reverse and backed out of the parking lot. Seconds later, they were on the road.

"What in the world happened?" Jackson asked once they'd cleared the Lockton city limits. Marsh wasn't surprised to note Jackson was heading toward Austin.

Marsh quickly filled Jackson in on the shooting event, then glanced back at Stacy, who was unusually quiet. "Anything to add?"

"No. You've covered it." Her voice was low and husky.

"You really think the gunman stumbled across your

car in the parking lot?" Jackson frowned. "How did he know you'd order room service?"

"Because Stacy is pregnant and he rightly assumed she'd need to eat." He rubbed his chin. "I should have anticipated that."

"How?" Jackson demanded. "Even if this guy had gotten your license plate, he shouldn't have been able to find you at the hotel."

With a sigh, he shrugged. "Yeah, well, he did. I think he bribed the room service clerk for information. And that means we need to take extreme measures to make sure we're not found again."

"I've arranged for a rental." Jackson glanced at him. "We'll pick that up in Austin. From there, I'm open to suggestions."

"Please don't call Tucker and Leanne." Stacy spoke for the first time since leaving the coffee shop. "I'm afraid this guy will assume we're all together."

As much as he'd wanted nothing more than to drop Stacy off with her brother and cop sister-in-law, he now was having second thoughts. The way they'd been found at the hotel bothered him. If the bad guys had run his plates, they could easily find out he was a Texas Ranger.

Marsh turned in his seat to look at her. "Are you absolutely sure you don't want to stay with them?"

"Yes, I'm sure." Her gaze didn't waver. "Please, Marsh. I feel safe with you."

Her words were like a punch to the gut. What if he wasn't up to the task? But then he forced a nod. "Okay then. We'll figure out a plan B."

"Good. Thank you."

He caught the arched expression on Jackson's face.

"We need to figure out a way to stay off the grid. And that means not using an SUV that's rented by a Texas Ranger."

Jackson blew out a breath. "Okay, but that makes things tricky. We can't rent a car without an ID."

"I know." Marsh tried to think of someone not associated with the rangers who could do that task for them.

"What if we ask Hank Feldman to rent the car for us?" Stacy suggested.

"No, sorry." Marsh shook his head. "That would be too obvious, as Hank lives right next door to you."

"I'll ask my Aunt Joyce Bellin to do it," Jackson offered. "She's technically not my aunt by blood, but an old friend of the family. I was raised to call her Aunt Joyce, and in some ways I'm closer to her than to my own family."

"Does she live in Austin?" Marsh asked.

"Yep." Jackson hit the Talk button on his steering wheel, then said, "Call Joyce."

A moment later the sound of a ringing phone echoed through the car. Joyce answered almost immediately. Marsh listened as Jackson and Joyce chatted for a minute before Jackson got down to his request. Thankfully, Joyce didn't hesitate.

"Of course I'll rent the SUV for you." She sounded excited at the prospect of helping them out. "I'll meet you there in twenty minutes."

"We'll be there, thanks." Jackson ended the call with a grin. "She's a sweetheart."

Marsh nodded, glad to have Aunt Joyce as an option. He needed to fill Tucker in on the recent events but thought it would be better to wait until they were in a replacement vehicle.

Which gave him another thought. "We need disposable phones, too."

"Yeah, I should have picked them up on the way." Jackson eyed the clock. "We'll have time to pick them up prior to meeting Joyce."

"Okay, thanks." Marsh relaxed into his seat. Things were moving in the right direction. When Jackson pulled up to a big box store, Marsh didn't hesitate to jump out. "I'll be back soon."

Having done this before, it didn't take him long to pick out the same phone brand he and his fellow rangers had used in the past. After paying with cash, he jogged back out to the car.

"Got them." He dropped the bag on the floor behind his seat, near the computer.

"Next stop, the rental agency," Jackson said.

The rental agency visit took a little longer. Jackson's aunt Joyce was a sweet, spry woman in her late fifties. Marsh and Stacy stayed in the car watching as the two greeted each other, then headed inside.

When they returned ten minutes later, Jackson held up the key fob. Then he kissed Aunt Joyce on the cheek and headed toward them.

"Give me a minute to drive the rental out of here, then we'll make the swap," Jackson said. "I asked Joyce to rent two cars for us. I'll use one from this point forward, too."

Marsh nodded, feeling blessed to have guys like Jackson covering his back.

Once Jackson pulled up in the first rental, the swap didn't take long. "What can I do to help?" Jackson asked when they were finished.

"Suggest a place for us to stay," Marsh said. "I know

you guys used a hotel when Tucker was in trouble and I was at the ranch protecting Stacy and Pops. I assume you paid in cash without an issue?"

"Yeah, we used the Sun Valley Motel and paid in cash. There's a family restaurant across the street." Jackson flashed a grin. "No room service."

"That sounds good to me." Marsh glanced at Stacy, who sat waiting in the rental, then added, "Any chance you can follow up on those fingerprints from the insurance card? And maybe chat with the local cops about the shooting at the hotel?"

Jackson nodded. "Absolutely. I'll do both of those things and then meet up with you at the motel."

"Thanks." Marsh took a moment to make sure Jackson had the numbers for their new disposable phones. When that was finished, he slid behind the wheel, started the engine and put the car in gear. As he drove away from the rental car agency, he told himself they were as far off grid as humanly possible.

And silently prayed his efforts were good enough to keep Stacy and her unborn child safe from harm.

# FIVE

Stacy felt better once the car rental agency was behind them. She drew in a deep breath and struggled to relax.

Stress was not good for the baby.

The danger was over, and she silently prayed it would stay that way. She didn't want to crawl through another window or walk through the city streets to escape a gunman.

Or to put Marsh in a position of having to shoot someone. Oh, she understood that was part of his job. But this time he'd done so to protect her. And that made her feel responsible.

"We're heading to a place called the Sun Valley Motel," Marsh said, breaking into her thoughts. "Tucker and Leanne used it back when they were on the run."

"That sounds good." She wasn't about to argue. Besides, she was oddly comforted by the fact that Tuck and Leanne had used the place. If her brother had thought it was safe, then she was sure they'd be fine staying there.

"We'll call Tuck once we're settled and have the new phones up and running. Jackson will meet up with us in a little while, too." Marsh reached over to cover her hand briefly with his. "We're going to be okay."

"I know." She managed a weak smile. "Like I said, I feel safe with you."

Marsh frowned but didn't say anything in response. After a moment, he removed his hand to fiddle with the temperature control. Had her comment placed undue pressure on him? As a Texas Ranger, he faced danger on a regular basis, the same way her brother did.

But she doubted Marsh had ever been in a position of protecting a pregnant woman before now.

They rode in silence for several minutes. She had been to Austin in the past, but not since she'd been married. These days, her life revolved around her job, her family—meaning Tucker, Leanne and Pops at the ranch—and OB appointments.

Thinking of them reminded her of the two men who showed up at the ranch looking for her. "Who do you think they were?" When Marsh shot her a puzzled look, she added, "Those men in suits who showed up on the ranch. We never got a chance to talk to Tucker and Leanne about that."

"Good point. We need all the information we can get." He executed a series of turns that had them heading in the opposite direction.

It was her turn to look confused. "Where is the Sun Valley Motel?"

"South of the city." He waved at the highway stretched before them. "We're taking the scenic route."

As in driving out of their way to make sure they weren't being followed. She appreciated his taking extra precautions and settled back in her seat. A wave of exhaustion hit her hard.

Marsh noticed her yawn. "Close your eyes and rest," he urged. "You're suffering from an adrenaline crash."

"I know what it's called." She had experienced it in the past, during the shootout on the ranch back in September. What she was going through was more than just the adrenaline, though. Being pregnant meant she was always feeling tired these days. "I'll be fine."

Twenty minutes later, Marsh pulled into the Sun Valley Motel parking lot. She gratefully slid out of the passenger seat, arching her back to stretch her muscles.

"Are you okay?" Marsh looked at her with concern.

"Of course." She didn't want to mention that the walking they'd done fleeing the hotel was the most exercise she'd done in a while. Her fault. She needed to be in better shape moving forward.

"Let's go." Marsh removed the star badge from his chest and stuck it into his pocket. She was curious as to why he'd done that, but there wasn't time to ask. He took a moment to sling the computer case over his shoulder and snag the bag of phones before reaching for her hand. "Let me do the talking, okay?"

She nodded. It felt strange to walk into the motel as if they were a couple. Rather than introduce himself as a Texas Ranger, he smiled wearily at the woman. "We need a room, but our credit cards were stolen. As you can see, my wife is pregnant and we are in desperate need for a place to stay."

"Oh, you poor thing." There was a distinct Texas drawl in the woman's tone. "I can take cash." She lowered her voice. "Even though I'm not supposed to."

"Thanks. You're a lifesaver." Marsh flashed his handsome smile, which clearly melted the clerk's heart. "My wife has been through a lot these days."

Stacy managed a weak smile, doing her best to play the role of an exhausted wife. The exhaustion part was easy.

It was the thought of being Marsh's wife that caused her heart to skip a beat.

A ridiculous response, as she'd made a promise to herself not to marry again after learning how Dan had lied about being fired. Now she knew he'd lied about way more important issues than that. She glanced at Marsh from beneath her lashes. Even though she knew he was a sweet, kind and honorable man, she wasn't interested in getting married again.

She'd be too busy raising her daughter to worry about her own social life. Or lack thereof.

"Thanks again." Marsh squeezed her hand. "This is a true blessing for us, isn't it, Marie?"

Marie? She nodded. "Yes, very much so." She couldn't come up with a different name for him as easily as he'd offered up hers, so she looked at the clerk. "Thank you for being so kind."

"Y'all just take care of yourself and that baby." The woman beamed at them. "Have a nice day."

"Thanks." Marsh tugged her back toward the door. "We're in room seven," he added in a low tone. "I'm sorry about not being able to get a suite or connecting rooms, but I didn't want to go that route, fearing that would draw too much attention."

"I understand." And the fact that he'd played the role of her doting husband explained why he wanted to do the talking. "You could have warned me," she added in a whisper as they walked back outside to get to their room. "I was caught off guard by your cover story."

Marsh flushed. "Sorry, you're right. I should have. I figured it was safer to provide a fake scenario than to use my badge to obtain the room."

"And it worked." After he unlocked the door, she stepped inside. The room was clean and had two queen beds. It felt much smaller than their suite, but safety trumped everything. "This is nice."

Marsh grunted as he set the laptop case on the small table, then rummaged in the bag containing their new phones. He opened the packaging. "We'll call Tucker as soon as I get these up and running."

She nodded and sank down on the edge of the bed closest to the bathroom. The hour was barely ten thirty in the morning, but it felt as if the day should be half over.

The process of getting the phones working didn't take as long as she'd anticipated. Marsh came over to sit beside her on the end of the bed. When he entered Tucker's phone number, her brother immediately answered.

"Who is this?" Tuck asked sharply.

"Marsh and Stacy. Your sister is fine, she's sitting right next to me," Marsh said quickly. "We aren't hurt, but a gunman did show up at our hotel in Lockton."

"How were you found?" Tuck demanded.

"I believe the shooter who followed us from Stacy's home got my license plate number and somehow tracked us to the hotel. He knew the staff wouldn't give out our room number, so he paid a room service employee to provide information." Marsh held Stacy's gaze. "Between me being a ranger with my star on my chest and Stacy's pregnancy, we were easy to identify. Don't worry, we've taken precautions at our new location."

There was a long pause as her brother digested that. "Where are you now?"

"Tuck, I think it's better if you stay out of this," Marsh said. "I have Jackson backing me up, but you need to stay focused on protecting Leanne and Pops."

"I take it Stacy told you about Leanne's pregnancy," Tucker said.

"Yeah." Marsh glanced at her. "And, look, it's probably better for us to stay away from you and to remain off grid as much as possible."

"I agree," Stacy said, speaking loud enough for Tucker to hear her. "Marsh has been doing an amazing job protecting me."

"I'm glad. And, yeah, I guess that's the best approach." Her brother's voice was husky with emotion. "It's a lot harder to stay objective when you know an unborn child is involved."

There was a long moment of silence before Marsh asked, "Tuck, does Leanne have any more information on the guys who showed up at the Rocking T?"

"I'm here, Marsh," Leanne said. "Tuck has the call on speaker. I wish I could give you more information, but they claimed to be from the federal government and flashed their creds so quickly I couldn't read their names or even which agency they were supposedly with. When I demanded names and to see their badges more closely, they got annoyed. One was tall, the same height as Tucker, but more husky in build. Not fat, but not thin, either. He had dark hair and wore reflector sunglasses, so I couldn't see his eyes. The other man was three inches shorter, so maybe five feet ten inches tall. He was lean with a runner's build, but his light brown hair was thinning on top, which gave me the impression he may have been older. But since he was also wearing reflector sunglasses, I can't accurately guess their ages. They wore black suits with white shirts and muted black ties. That part did scream 'fed.' But from which agency, I have no clue."

"You have a good eye for detail, Leanne." Marsh sounded impressed. "What happened when you pressed for more information?"

"They told me to cooperate or they would be back with a search warrant." Her tone sounded annoyed. "I told them to go ahead and come back with their warrant, because I wasn't talking to anyone who refused to properly identify themselves. They seemed surprised but then turned and left without another word." A hint of satisfaction tinged her tone. "They must have realized they messed with the wrong woman."

"Leanne called me right after that. She helped get Pops out of there." Tucker picked up the story. "I asked our neighbor to help with the livestock while we're gone."

"Okay, thanks. I still think that's odd," Marsh said. "I mean, why would someone from the federal government want to talk to Stacy?"

"I don't know," Tucker admitted. "But considering how they refused to allow Leanne to closely examine their creds, I doubt they were legit."

Stacy swallowed hard, feeling sick all over again. Bad enough to know the knife man was after her, but two other men in suits pretending to be feds?

Maybe Marsh wasn't too far off base with his theory of domestic terrorism.

\* \* \*

When the blood drained from Stacy's face, Marsh quickly ended the call with Tuck and Leanne. He tossed the phone aside and slipped his arm around Stacy's waist.

"Hey, are you okay?"

She shook her head slowly. "Hearing Leanne describe her encounter with the two men at the ranch was awful." She lifted her tortured gaze to his. "What if you're right about this being a bigger deal than a simple stolen code? What if Dan was involved in something big and terrible?"

He kicked himself for offering that theory yesterday. Even if domestic terrorism was a distinct possibility, she didn't need the additional stress of thinking about it. "I don't know what code Dan stole, but I'm leaning toward bank accounts of some sort or corporate espionage." He offered a reassuring smile. "Trust me, we're going to get to the truth. The gunman already made one mistake by allowing me a shot back at the hotel. Jackson is heading over now to talk to the local police about the incident. He'll fill us in on what he learns."

"He is?" The frank hope in her bright blue eyes made him wish he could do more for her. "I hope I recognize his name once we know what it is."

"Me too." He hugged her. "Jackson was also going to follow up on the insurance card he retrieved from your car. Maybe running the fingerprints will provide some answers."

"I pray it will." Stacy leaned against him, resting her head on his shoulder. "I'm so glad you're here."

Red warning lights flashed in the back of his mind. Holding Stacy like this was treading on dangerous ground. He liked and respected her.

And cared about her far more than he should.

Reminding himself she was Tucker's little sister and pregnant didn't seem to help. Not when she nestled against him like this.

Yet he couldn't find the will to pull away. He simply held her close, determined to be there for her.

"Marsh?" She lifted her head to look up at him. She was so close he could have easily kissed her. But of course he wouldn't betray her trust like that.

"What's wrong?" He searched her gaze. "Are you feeling okay? The baby…" He didn't know how to ask if she was experiencing discomfort.

"I'm fine. Better now that I'm with you." Her gaze was so intense, his mouth went dry and his brain synapses seemed to stop working. "I wish—"

Her wish was cut off by the shrill ring from their new disposable cell phone. Knowing the only people who had the number were Jackson and Tucker, he turned to grab it.

Stacy moved away, running a hand through her long dark hair as if she'd been shaken by their embrace, too.

"Branson," he answered curtly. His skin felt hot and flushed, and it was all he could do not to toss the phone aside to pull Stacy back into his arms. Why he was struck by the sudden need to kiss her, he had no clue.

"It's Jackson. I'm on my way."

"Okay." Marsh hoped he sounded casual as he rose to his feet. He turned so that he could face Stacy as he spoke to Jackson. "We spoke to Tucker and Leanne, too. I'll fill you in when you get here."

"Great. And I'll do the same. The reason I called is to ask if you and Stacy are hungry. I figured I could stop to pick up lunch along the way."

"Are you obsessed with food now, too?" Tucker was usually the one to keep track of their mealtimes.

"Hey, I'm only thinking of Tucker's baby sister who, as you pointed out earlier, is pregnant and needs to eat." A hint of defensiveness lined Jackson's voice. "Besides, you guys had breakfast. I did not."

"Yeah, okay. Lunch sounds good." He glanced at Stacy. "What would you like?"

She stroked her hand over her belly as she considered her options. "Don't laugh, but I would love a cheeseburger with extra pickles."

"I'm not laughing." Even though her request did make him smile. "We'll take two cheeseburgers with extra pickles and fries," he said to Jackson.

"And a chocolate shake," Stacy added. "Extra calcium is good for the baby."

"Did you get that? Add a chocolate shake to the order for the baby. Thanks, Jackson." Marsh lowered the phone and glanced around the motel room. "I'll set up the computer so we can get some work done this afternoon."

"That sounds good." Stacy hadn't moved from her perch on the end of the bed. She appeared lost in thought, and he hoped she wasn't overthinking their embrace.

The way he was, he silently admitted.

Stacy rose and disappeared into the bathroom. He opened the computer, then decided against logging into the local internet connection. Staying off grid meant not using the internet. At least for a while.

Then he glanced at the bathroom door, hoping she wasn't crying in there, but when she emerged a few minutes later, there was no evidence of recent tears.

"Hey, do I get to be the baby's Uncle Marsh?" he asked, trying to lighten the mood.

"Ah, sure if you'd like." Stacy avoided his direct gaze in a way that indicated she wasn't keen on the idea. "I wouldn't mind some help in picking out her name. I'm struggling a bit, going back and forth between a few options."

He was surprised by that. Both that she hadn't decided on a name and that she cared enough to ask his opinion. "I thought you had a name already picked out."

She shrugged. "Like I said, I keep going back and forth. My mother's name was Eleanor. I like it, but I'm not sure if it's smart to name a baby after her dead grandmother."

"Eleanor is a beautiful name." He smiled. "I think it's a nice way to honor your mother."

"Yeah, maybe. I guess I'll keep Eleanor either as a first or middle name." She crossed over to where he had the computer open on the desk. "Do you mind if I check a few of my programs? I would like to make sure Dan didn't imbed the code in them."

"Have at it." Marsh stood and gestured for her to take the chair. "What kind of programs?"

"I figured I should check my email more closely, examine our banking software and, most importantly, the malware program." She glanced up at him over her shoulder. "I think I'll start with the malware program first since cybersecurity was Dan's area of expertise."

"Can you check that if you're offline?" He put a hand on her arm to stop her from using the keyboard. "Because I don't think we should connect to the local internet just yet."

That made her frown. "I can start by checking the programs while offline, but I'll need to get on the internet at some point."

Was he being overly paranoid? Maybe. "Stay offline for now." His new phone rang again, and this time he recognized Jackson's number. "Yeah?"

"What room?" Jackson asked. "I'm in the parking lot."

"Room seven. I'll meet you at the door." Marsh lowered the phone and crossed over to let Jackson in. His buddy carried two large bags of fast food. The scent of warm fries filled the air, making his stomach growl.

Maybe he was obsessed with food, too.

"Let's eat first," Jackson said. "I can think better on a full stomach."

Stacy shut the laptop and moved it out of the way so Jackson could set the bags down. There wasn't enough room for all of them to fit around the table, so he and Jackson sat on the beds, leaving Stacy to have the table.

She rummaged in the bags and handed out their meals. Then she clasped her hands together and bowed her head. "Dear Lord Jesus, we thank You for this food we are about to eat. We ask that You continue to keep us safe in Your care. Amen."

"Amen," he and Jackson echoed.

Stacy took a long slurp from her chocolate shake before digging into her meal. He and Jackson exchanged a glance as they ate, too. He could tell that Jackson had news and was suddenly glad his buddy had suggested they eat first. It was important for Stacy to make sure the baby received the nourishment she needed.

"Did you go to the hotel crime scene?" Stacy asked after a few minutes of silence.

"Yeah. The local cops didn't find anyone at the scene." Jackson eyed Marsh. "Just a bunch of bullets and some blood."

That surprised him. "No body?"

"Nope." Jackson munched a fry. "Seems the perp got away."

"Will they run DNA tests on the blood?" Marsh asked.

"I personally requested that." Jackson nodded. "They agreed but said it would take time."

"Yeah, time we don't have," Marsh said glumly.

Stacy grimaced and nodded. "I guess we can't be too upset he's not dead."

Marsh was rather upset at that news but kept the thought to himself. They ate for another few minutes in silence, until Stacy had finished her burger and half her fries.

Sitting back in her chair, she sipped on the chocolate shake, eyeing Jackson. "Okay, what else did you find out? I can tell there's more to this."

Jackson sighed. "You're a lot like your brother. The lab called to let me know they ran the fingerprints found on the insurance card. They belong to a man by the name of Damien Colter."

Stacy went pale. "Damien Colter? My husband's real name is Damien Colter? Not Daniel Copeland?"

"I'm afraid so," Jackson said. "I'm sorry."

Marsh instantly crossed to her side, dropped down beside her and wrapped a protective arm around her shoulders, inwardly railing at the dead man who'd done this to her.

Not only had Dan, aka Damien—who'd sworn to love her—lied about his real identity, but it appeared as if those same lies had put Stacy in the center of danger.

# SIX

Stacy leaned against Marsh, struggling with the fact that the man she'd married, the father of her child was a stranger. Not just a stranger, but likely a criminal! Why else would Dan have changed his name?

Had their marriage even been legal? They'd stood in church and promised to love and cherish one another. Had that been a lie? And if so, why had Dan bothered to marry her in the first place?

*Why, Lord, why?* She squeezed her eyes against the sting of tears.

"I'm sorry," Marsh murmured, his mouth near her ear. "I'm sorry you're going through this."

She tried to blink away the tears, but it was no use. A sob ripped free, and she turned to bury her face against Marsh's chest as she broke down.

Once she allowed the tears to fall, it seemed they would never stop. She had cried after Dan had been murdered, but this was different.

She was crying for something that she'd never had in the first place. A loving husband. A wonderful marriage. A true partner.

Everything was a lie!

"It's okay, I'm here." Marsh didn't tell her to stop crying. He simply smoothed his hand down her back and held her close. "You have every right to be upset."

Ironically, his words helped her wrestle her emotions under control. Yes, she had a right to be upset, but there were plenty of people out there who had less than she did. She'd met one woman at the widow support group who had lost her husband and her son. And Harold Green had lost his wife of thirty years. She was alive and had her baby. What more could she ask for?

She drew in several deep, ragged breaths and sniffled loudly.

Marsh pressed a wad of tissues into her hand. His thoughtfulness almost turned the waterworks back on, but she managed to hold them back. Nodding her thanks, she lifted her head and wiped at her face. Then blew her nose.

No doubt she looked like a wreck. Not that it should matter, but she rose on shaky legs. "Excuse me." She turned and hurried into the bathroom.

Splashing cold water on her face helped. She blew her nose again and stared at her blotchy complexion reflected in the mirror. No pretty crying for her. She looked worse than she'd anticipated. And why she cared what Marsh thought of her looks was a mystery. It shouldn't matter. He was her brother's friend, nothing more.

She took another moment to press a cold washcloth against her puffy eyes, then set it aside.

Okay, so Dan, or Damien, had lied to her. Her gaze dropped to her pregnant belly, and she pressed her palms against the baby resting there. All that mattered now was staying alive and creating a new life for her daughter.

Feeling better, she turned and joined Jackson and

Marsh. Only Jackson wasn't there. She frowned. "Where's Jackson?"

"He headed out to get some bottled water for you." Marsh rose and eyed her thoughtfully. "We're going to get through this. I'll be here and will support you."

"I know." Despite her new trust issues, she believed Marsh. He'd proven himself determined to protect her over and over since this nightmare started. And she humbly knew he would sacrifice his life for hers if necessary.

She desperately prayed it wouldn't come to that. For Marsh or Jackson. Or anyone else for that matter.

*Please Lord Jesus, guide us and keep us all safe in Your care!*

The prayer brought a renewed sense of calmness washing over her. She felt stronger knowing God was watching over them, too. And she needed to remember to lean on her faith in times of trouble. "I'm sorry to break down like that." She forced a smile. "I guess it's just—been a rough day."

"You're a remarkably strong woman, Stacy." His dark brown eyes reflected admiration. "I think you've been holding yourself together exceptionally well."

Now he was making her blush. Time to change the subject. "Okay, so now that we know Dan's real name is Damien Colter, how does that help us figure out what the code is? And who Damien stole it from? And who he really was, for that matter?"

Before Marsh could answer, the motel room door opened to reveal Jackson standing there with a six pack of bottled water. He looked relieved that she wasn't crying any longer as he set it on the table. "Hey. I thought you might need to drink something."

Marsh pulled a bottle from the pack, twisted the cap off and handed it to her. She took a long gulp, realizing they were right. All that crying had caused her to feel dehydrated. "Thank you."

"Anytime." Jackson waved that off and tossed the room key card on the table.

"I was just asking Marsh where we go from here." She sat back on the edge of the bed. "Can we figure out why Damien changed his name?" She decided to refer to the man who'd lied to her as Damien from now on, since that was his real name. And it helped to remind her that the man she'd married hadn't really existed.

"We know a little bit." Marsh sat next to her again, as if worried she might fall apart. "We know that Damien Colter was in the Witness Protection Program, generally referred to as WITSEC. It's run, as you know, by the US Marshals Service."

"The rest of his file is sealed," Jackson added. "I made a call to a guy by the name of Noel Harrington. He was Damien's US Marshal contact. I haven't heard back from him, yet."

"I don't know that we're going to learn much from Harrington." Marsh frowned. "If the US Marshals Service had created this new identity of Dan Copeland, then the background check would have been solid as a rock. As it stands now, the guy's background has holes in it. Dan Copeland popped into existence when he was eighteen, with nothing existing prior. Not even a birth certificate."

A chill settled over her. "Does that mean he left the WITSEC program? Maybe because he'd refused to testify as promised?"

"That's one theory," Marsh agreed. "There could be

others. The main issue is that the US Marshals Service would have created a thorough backstory for him. Complete with all necessary documents if he was still under their protection."

"That makes sense." She told herself it didn't matter if Damien was a criminal or innocent. The end result was the same.

He'd stolen something important enough that he'd been murdered.

They had one piece of the puzzle. She silently prayed that they'd learn more soon.

And put an end to this nightmare once and for all.

The way Stacy had pulled herself together after learning the devastating truth was amazing.

As if Marsh needed another reason to admire her.

He knew he was getting emotionally involved with her and that he needed to keep a professional distance between them to protect her. Emotions could cloud a man's judgment, and he'd never forgive himself if he failed her.

Yet he couldn't bear the thought of handing Stacy over to someone else. He was personally invested in seeing this through. In protecting Stacy.

And her unborn child.

When Jackson's phone rang, they all jumped. Talk about being on edge.

"It's an unknown number," Jackson said as he swiped the phone screen to answer it. "This is Ranger Jackson Woodlow." After a brief pause, Jackson said, "Thanks for getting back to me so quickly. I'd like to place this call on speaker so Ranger Marshall Branson can hear this."

The US Marshal must have agreed, because Jackson

lowered the phone and pressed a button. Then he held it out in front of him. "Marshal Harrington, what can you tell us about Damien Colter?"

"Just call me Noel," the man's gruff voice said. "Kinda confusing since you have a ranger named Marshall."

"Okay, Noel," Marsh said with a wry smile. "You can call me Marsh, it's easier and less confusing. We need to understand what Damien Colter was involved with back when he entered the program, because his widow is in danger, and we have reason to believe the threat against her could be connected to his past."

"Well, now, I don't see how that's possible," Noel said. "Damien was twenty-six when he died. Ten years is a long time."

"I understand, but we'd still like to know what's going on."

There was a long pause before Noel Harrington spoke. "If you really think Damien's widow is in danger, then we should meet in person. It's a lot to discuss over the phone."

Marsh locked gazes with Jackson. It seemed odd to him that Noel Harrington wanted to meet in person. Then again, maybe whatever Damien had been involved in was something sensitive in nature.

He thought again about the two men in black suits who'd shown up at the Rocking T Ranch looking for Stacy. Feds? Homeland Security?

Someone else?

"Look, it's not that I don't want to help," Noel said, as if reading their thoughts. "I just think that's a conversation better had in person. Do you have time to meet later this afternoon? Or early tomorrow morning?"

"This afternoon, say three o'clock?" Marsh frowned,

considering a neutral location. He decided to use the same coffee shop they'd visited earlier. "We can meet you at the Corner Coffee Café in Austin."

"I can make that work," Noel agreed. "See you then."

Jackson ended the call and slid his phone back into his pocket. "I wonder what's so important he can't discuss it over the phone."

Marsh glanced at Stacy, who was eyeing him curiously. "You think it's something related to homeland security."

"I think it's probably related to the government in some way," he agreed.

Her eyes widened. "You don't think the government killed him?"

"No, that's not likely," Marsh hastened to reassure her. "For one thing, even if they'd known Damien stole some important computer code, they'd have arrested him and thrown him in jail. They wouldn't kill him and steal his computer."

"You're right." Stacy looked relieved.

"The part of this that bothers me the most is the way the two so-called Feds showed up at the ranch. I'm sure they were looking for the code. But why not show their credentials to Leanne?"

"Maybe they're not feds, but are the rightful owners of the code," Jackson suggested.

"Maybe." Marsh turned toward Stacy, gesturing to the laptop computer. "Maybe we should take some time to go through your programs to make sure Damien didn't hide them in there."

"I'm happy to try." She hesitated. "It would be easier to do that with internet access, though. If we don't want to use the connection here, maybe we should find another spot instead?"

"Good idea." He glanced at his watch. They had two hours before their three-o'clock meeting time. "We can head to the Corner Coffee Café early. Having glass windows on two sides of the building will enable us to see anyone coming."

Jackson nodded. "I like it."

"Good." Marsh turned and quickly tucked the computer in the carrying case. Slinging the strap over his shoulder and pocketing the key card, he added, "Let's hit the road."

Jackson opened the door, glanced around and then gave him the okay sign.

"Go ahead, Stacy." He indicated she should follow him. "We'll take our rental."

She nodded. He dug the key fob from his pocket and unlocked the door. Jackson's vehicle was parked in a spot two spaces to the right.

"You may as well ride with us," Marsh told him as he opened the passenger side door for Stacy.

"I think we should take both vehicles just in case." Jackson shrugged. "I'll drive around the neighborhood while you work."

The extra layer of protection was a good idea, so Marsh nodded in agreement. He stored the laptop on the floor at Stacy's feet, then slid behind the wheel.

The trip to the Corner Coffee Café didn't take too long. Marsh didn't see anything remotely suspicious, so he didn't bother with too many turns. After circling the block, he pulled into the small parking lot and chose a spot toward the back.

After grabbing the computer, he escorted Stacy inside. Their corner table was open, so he swiftly nabbed it. He set up the computer for Stacy, then went over to buy coffee for him and water for Stacy.

She was hard at work by the time he returned. He wanted to watch her but decided his job was to watch the intersection outside instead.

It was boring surveillance work, but he forced himself to take note of the cars going past. In the middle of the day, traffic was steady. He tried to make sure the same car didn't pass by several times, but that was no easy task.

Pickup trucks were popular in Texas, and he'd lost count of how many drove by. But he tried to notice specifics of each vehicle just in case.

A Texas A&M bumper sticker on one, a University of Texas sticker on another. College football was a big deal in this town.

Some trucks had dents or scrapes. He watched as a black SUV rolled past. The vehicle looked almost brand new, much like his rental.

Then he realized that had been Jackson, driving around the neighborhood as promised. Marsh physically relaxed, but maintained his vigilant surveillance.

"Nothing on my malware program." Stacy sighed and took a sip of her water. "I'll check my email next."

"Take your time." According to his watch, they still had another ninety minutes before their scheduled meeting with Noel Harrington.

She nodded and turned her attention back to the screen. He continued watching traffic. He'd anticipated seeing Jackson's SUV again, but for several minutes nobody drove past.

His phone rang. Recognizing Jackson's number, he answered without hesitation. "Hey, Jackson."

"Hey, I'm across the street in the strip mall parking lot," Jackson said. "Did you see that black SUV going by?"

Marsh straightened. "Yes. I thought it was you?"

"Not me, but I didn't get a good view of the driver. I was wondering if it might have been Noel Harrington checking the place out."

"Yeah. Gotta admit, I would have done the same thing," Marsh agreed. "He never did mention where he was coming in from."

"No, he didn't." Jackson was quiet for a moment. "I'll stay out here while you and Stacy meet with him."

"Thanks. I'll update you when we're finished." Marsh eyed the strip mall parking lot. "I see your rental. It's not directly across from the café, but close enough."

"Yep. Too bad I don't have a pair of binocs with me," Jackson said.

"It won't matter since we don't know what Noel Harrington looks like." Marsh turned his gaze away from Jackson's SUV to watch the cars again. "Stay in touch. I'll give you the high sign when Noel arrives. If he did a drive by, I have a feeling he'll be early." Again, being the first to arrive at a meeting location was something Marsh would do.

"Okay. Later." Jackson ended the call.

The next thirty minutes dragged by with excruciating slowness. Easier for Stacy, as she was immersed in her work. Marsh had to force himself to pay attention to the traffic outside rather than watching her.

She was beautiful, the way her skin glowed and her

dark hair waved softly around her face. Her beauty seemed enhanced by her pregnancy.

Or maybe it was just that he was looking at her differently now that she wasn't married.

Enough. He frowned when he saw a black SUV driving slowly past the café. He hit the redial to reach Jackson. "Did you see that?"

"Yeah. I only caught a glimpse of the plate, the first two numbers were eight-four." There was a pause. "I didn't catch the license of the first SUV, though."

He hadn't, either. "That's fine. We'll just make sure this particular SUV doesn't swing past the café again. There's no reason for Noel Harrington to keep driving by the place, right?"

"Right," Jackson agreed. "Stay alert."

"You too." Marsh lowered his phone. For some reason, he didn't like this. What if the first SUV they'd spotted didn't belong to Noel Harrington? Then again, the SUV could belong to just about anyone. No reason to be threatened by it.

Yet he couldn't just sit there, waiting. His gut instincts were screaming at him. He stood and reached for the computer case. "I think you may need to log off."

"Why?" She looked confused.

"I'm not sure we're staying." He couldn't explain the sense of unease that dogged him.

Stacy glanced around the room, then rose to her feet. She closed the laptop. "Okay, but I'm not sure why we need to leave."

He didn't answer, still scanning the street outside, just as the black SUV made another appearance.

His phone jangled and he knew Jackson was calling

a warning. Marsh shoved the computer into the case and caught Stacy's hand. He'd dragged her halfway across the room toward the corner restrooms when the glass window shattered beneath the force of gunfire.

# SEVEN

Why did this keep happening? Stacy curled her shoulders inward, staying as close to Marsh as possible while he half dragged her through the coffee shop and out a back door. She hadn't remembered the rear exit being there, but Marsh must have noticed it being near the restrooms the last time they were here.

Once again, his foresight and his keen law enforcement instincts had kept her safe.

"The SUV is over there." Marsh jutted his chin to the back of the parking lot. She remembered wondering why he'd parked so far away from the main entrance.

Now she knew.

She walked as quickly as possible to their rental. Marsh opened the passenger door for her, dropped the laptop on the floor and then raced around to the driver's seat. Seconds later they were on the move. The SUV rocked jarringly from side to side as Marsh drove it up and over the curb to get through to the adjacent parking lot of a gas station. Then he did the same maneuver again to get through to the parking lot of a grocery store.

Stacy gripped the handrest tightly until Marsh was out on a street, driving away from the café. She tried to breathe normally, but her heart was racing. The sound of police sirens split the air. She imagined the officers converging on the Corner Coffee Café. Had anyone else been injured? She prayed everyone else who had been inside the café when the gunfire erupted was safe.

When Marsh's phone rang, he quickly pulled the device from his pocket and handed it to her.

"Hello?" Her voice sounded shaky to her own ears.

"It's Jackson. Are you and Marsh okay?"

"Yes. We're not hurt." At least, she didn't think Marsh had been hit. She raked her gaze over him, grateful she didn't see any blood. "Marsh took me out through the back. We're in the rental now, heading—uh—east?"

"Southeast," Marsh corrected. "Tell Jackson we need an alternate plan to meet with Harrington. I'm not convinced he didn't set us up back there."

She relayed the message.

"I thought of that, too," Jackson admitted. "Let's meet at a place called Smoky Joes. Marsh should know where it is, we've eaten there before."

"Smoky Joes," she repeated. When Marsh nodded, acknowledging the restaurant, she added, "Okay. We'll see you soon."

"Yeah. Soon." Jackson ended the call.

Stacy dropped the phone in the cupholder and suppressed a shiver that had nothing to do with the temperature. "You really think the US Marshal is involved?"

"Either he set us up or someone tracked your computer via the Wi-Fi connection." He met her gaze. "You tell me which one is more likely."

It was a tough question. Yet in the end, she didn't believe the marshal was dirty. "I think it must have been the computer connection." She glanced at the laptop he'd tossed on the floor at her feet. "You warned me against using the motel internet and your fears were justified. These bad guys must be more computer savvy than we realize."

Marsh shrugged. "Maybe. Or maybe we have another dirty cop on our hands."

"I find it hard to believe Noel is involved." She wasn't sure why she was sticking up for a man she'd never met. "For one thing, he couldn't have known we'd arrive at the coffee shop early. Secondly, why would he want us dead? If he really wanted the infamous code my husband stole, why not find a way to lure us in a more secluded location? Firing randomly into the coffee shop seems reckless."

"Yeah, I hate to admit you're right. Shooting at us through the window wasn't smart." Marsh's expression remained grim as he turned several corners, no doubt doing his best to make sure they weren't followed. "I agree that it's hard to believe the US Marshals Service would have someone on the inside working against them. The federal government does a good job of vetting their people. It's more rigorous than becoming a Texas Ranger, and that's saying something."

"Good to know." She sighed. "But if we're going to find the mystery code, we need to be online. I think there's a way to redirect the IP address on a computer to make it more difficult to track. I've never done that, but I'll see what I can do once we're settled in a new location."

"Okay." Marsh appeared to relax now that it was clear they'd gotten away from the coffee shop without being followed. "We'll discuss our next steps with Jackson. First and foremost, a better location to meet with Harrington."

"Sounds good." She smoothed her hands over her abdomen to calm herself and the baby. Now that they were safe, she couldn't help reliving those moments Marsh had dragged her away from the windows mere seconds before the gunfire rang out.

God was watching over them. If not for Marsh feeling antsy about sticking around, she very much feared the outcome would have been vastly different.

*Thank You, Lord Jesus!*

Smoky Joes was one of the many barbecue restaurants in the city. It looked like a nice place, and at this hour a good halfway between lunch and dinner it, wasn't too busy.

Marsh drove around to the back of the restaurant to find a parking spot. Then he turned so that he could back in for an easy escape. "Hold on a minute." He put a hand on her arm to stop her from releasing the seat belt. "I think that's Jackson over there."

She turned to see Jackson driving toward them. He pulled in alongside Marsh, and both men lowered their windows.

"Any chance you got a look at the driver?" Marsh asked.

"Nope." Jackson scowled. "I caught the same two digits, along with a third of the license plate, though. The first three numbers are 840."

"We can try to track it through the DMV database," Marsh said. "But I don't have high hopes we'll find the owner that easily. The vehicle could be a rental, like ours, or stolen."

"Yeah, but it's worth a shot." Jackson glanced at her. "I'm glad you're okay, Stacy."

"Thanks to you and Marsh." She tried to smile. "Smart of you to position yourself across the street at the strip mall."

The sound of a ringing phone made Jackson grimace. "That's probably Harrington. He may have seen the police response at the coffee shop."

She glanced at the clock on the dashboard. "He's early, there's still twenty-five minutes prior to our scheduled meeting."

"Yeah, well, he may have decided to show up early. The way we did." Jackson held up his phone. "I'll have to answer his call eventually. What would you like me to do?"

"We need a meeting spot that provides us an advantage," Marsh said. "And for the life of me, I can't come up with a viable option."

After what seemed like forever, Jackson's phone stopped ringing. The silence stretched to a full minute.

"We could meet with him at the state capitol office building," Jackson suggested. "The security is decent and we can get in early."

Marsh nodded. "I was just thinking the same thing. We'll meet in one of the conference rooms. After that, though, we need to secure a rental house. I don't want to be in a motel like the Sun Valley with only one way in or out of the rooms."

"Roger that. I'll see if Sam can work on that for us while we meet with Harrington." Jackson groaned when his phone rang again. "I'll tell Harrington to meet us there in an hour."

"We'll head over now." Marsh put car in Drive. "See you soon."

Jackson rolled up his window and answered the phone.

The trip to downtown Austin took a solid forty minutes. Traffic grew worse the closer they got to the capitol, reminding her why she preferred to live in San Antonio. As they moved at a snail's pace, she thought of her deceased husband. Was everything Damien had told her a lie? Or had there been some shred of truth intermingled in his stories? She hoped and prayed Noel Harrington would provide some answers.

After they reached the office building, Marsh parked the SUV. Jackson had been right about the extra layer of security. Marsh had to show his credentials more than once to gain access. After taking the elevator to the third floor, Marsh escorted her to a conference room.

"Would you like some water?" he asked.

"Yes, please."

He smiled. "I'll be back soon. I'm going to ask our tech expert, Nina, to see if she can help with your idea of rerouting the IP address of your laptop."

"Great." She eased into a chair. "That's something Dan, er, Damien would have been able to do."

Marsh returned a few minutes later with her bottle of water and a pretty redhead named Nina Hobson. "May I?" Nina gestured to the laptop.

"Have at it." Stacy pushed it forward.

"I'll be back soon." Nina smiled again before ducking from the room.

Ten minutes later, Jackson strode in. "Guess who's already downstairs? I think Harrington must have broken the speed limit to get here."

"No lie," Marsh muttered. "Okay, let's get this over with."

"I'll head down to grab him." Jackson disappeared, and shortly afterward, Nina returned with the laptop.

"All set." The tech's green eyes twinkled. "I have inserted a code to reroute the IP Address. If anyone tries to track it, they'll end up at the wrong location."

"Great." Stacy smiled. "Appreciate your help."

Moments later, Jackson returned with a man who appeared to be in his mid-fifties. "Noel Harrington?" Marsh asked reaching out to shake his hand. "Ranger Marsh Branson and this is Stacy Copeland."

She rose to shake Noel's hand, too.

"Jackson filled me in on the SUV and subsequent gunfire at the coffee shop." Noel got right down to business. "I assure you, I had nothing to do with that."

"Yeah, well, based on the timing so close to our meeting, you can't fault me for being suspicious." Marsh drummed his fingers on the table. "We've taken precautions to make sure we're not tracked again."

"Good." Noel switched his attention to her. "Did your husband mention his father?"

She eyed him curiously. "Only to tell me his parents died when he was in college. Not that we were able to find any records proving he even attended college," she added.

Noel didn't look surprised. "Ten years ago, when Damien was sixteen, he and his father, Geoff Colter, hacked into the database of the Department of Defense. When they were arrested, Damien agreed to testify against his father in exchange for serving no jail time and being placed in Witness Protection."

Stacy stared at Noel, dumbfounded. The Department of Defense? Her husband had actually breached the highest level of government when he was only sixteen years old?

Her mind whirled with possibilities. Was that original hacking crime part of the reason she was in danger now?

Or had her late husband recently hacked into a different database, accessing and stealing a different code?

One thing was for sure. Even if Damien hadn't attended college, it was clear his computer skills were even better than she'd realized.

And that could not be good.

Marsh watched as a myriad of expressions crossed Stacy's features as Noel Harrington explained about how Damien had been arrested alongside his father ten years ago for hacking into the Defense Department's database.

That a sixteen-year-old had pulled that off seemed incredible.

"What happened? Why didn't Damien cooperate with the investigation?" Marsh asked.

Noel glanced at him and nodded. "You noticed that Dan Copeland didn't exist prior to his obtaining a driver's license at the age of eighteen. What happened is that someone tried to kill Damien a week before the trial. Damien was seventeen by then, and he managed to escape from the hospital after being grazed by a bullet." A frown marred Noel's forehead. "That's on us. We dropped the ball. Suffice it to say that Damien disappeared. Without his testimony, we didn't have enough evidence against his father, Geoff Colter. That forced us to drop the charges and to release him."

Stacy's expression turned incredulous. "You're saying the entire Marshals Service couldn't find them?"

Noel's face flushed. "I know we messed up. We should have found Damien. And we shouldn't have lost track of his father. We had a team on Geoff, but the guy changed his appearance and managed to escape. He and his son dropped off the radar."

Marsh frowned. "You believe Geoff Colter is alive?"

"We're not sure what to think." Noel sighed heavily. "Geoff wasn't happy that Damien turned against him, so we don't believe they stayed together. Now that Damien has been murdered, we strongly believe Geoff may be alive and has extracted revenge against his son."

"How did they find each other after all this time?" The pieces of the puzzle weren't fitting together from what Marsh could tell. "Were Damien and Geoff originally from this area?"

"No, they lived in Iowa," Noel said.

"That's why Damien told me he went to Iowa State," Stacy said. "Maybe that was the college he wanted to attend, until he and his dad were arrested."

"That's possible," Noel agreed. "I know for a fact Damien's mother died when he was only five, and his father raised him. Damien told us that his father taught him everything he knew about computer hacking."

"Some legacy," Marsh said wryly. "How did they both end up here in Texas?"

"I don't know for sure that Geoff Colter is here, but obviously Damien found a job here and then got married." Noel darted a glance at Stacy. "Damien's murder has revived the old case against his father. We think his death could be related to his original agreement to testify against his father."

"Or Damien got involved in something else." A hint of bitterness laced Stacy's tone. "The man who held me at knifepoint wanted the code Damien had stolen. Maybe

I'm overthinking it, but it sounded like the theft was recent."

Noel looked surprised. "When did that happen?"

Marsh filled him in on the multiple attempts on Stacy's life. Including the most recent gunfire at the Corner Coffee Café.

"We can place Stacy in Witness Protection," Noel offered.

"No thanks." Marsh wasn't about to trust the guy that far. "She's not a witness, she's a victim."

"I'd rather stay with Marsh and Jackson," Stacy added. "They've been doing a great job of keeping me safe."

"But if Geoff Colter is the one behind these attempts—" Noel began, but Marsh cut him off.

"Stacy is staying with me. End of story." He held the marshal's gaze. "What else can you tell us about this Geoff Colter? Do you have photos of him?"

"They're ten years old, but I can get them to you." Harrington seemed to realize their interview was over. He turned toward Stacy. "Can you remember anything else about what Damien was doing prior to his death? Anything that would explain where this mystery code of his has been hidden?"

Marsh subtly shook his head. Stacy seemed to understand that this wasn't the time to go into detail about what they had and hadn't found. "I'm sorry, but I have no idea. When the guy held me at knifepoint, I pretended the code was in the office so I could escape. My husband was acting a little weird prior to his death, but I don't know anything about a code."

Noel looked disappointed. "Okay, but please reach out

to me if you remember anything. Even the smallest detail could be important."

"What are you doing to find Geoff Colter?" Marsh asked. "Do you have any other suspects in mind for who may have killed Damien?"

"No. I wish I did." Noel sighed again. "His father is at the top of the suspect list. The issue is that we know the Colters' original plan was to sell the DOD information on the dark web. We don't know anything about who their buyer might have been."

Marsh found it hard to imagine that Damien's murder was related to a crime from ten years ago. But that was Harrington's problem. Not his.

His job was to keep Stacy and her unborn child safe while searching her programs for the code. He hated to consider the very real possibility that Damien had hidden the code somewhere else. Someplace where nobody would find it.

"Well, thanks for agreeing to meet." Noel reluctantly rose to his feet. It was clear the US Marshal had hoped to learn more information from Stacy related to her deceased husband.

Instead, the flow of information had been the other way around.

"We'll walk you out." Marsh decided it would be better for them to leave at the same time. In truth, he'd prefer to hit the road before Noel did. Just to be extra cautious.

"I, um, have to use the restroom, first." Stacy looked embarrassed and he kicked himself again for not anticipating her needs.

"We'll wait." He gestured to the restrooms that were

located halfway down the hall. "I have a few more questions for Noel."

Marsh picked up the computer case as Stacy slipped away.

"What kind of questions?" Noel sounded irritated.

"Exactly what data was stolen from DOD?" Marsh asked. "Is that data still relevant today?"

Noel shrugged. "In my honest opinion? That's not likely. I don't know the details, other than the Colters stole some highly sensitive military information. After the breach was discovered, the military went to great lengths to mitigate the damage."

"Okay, so the missing code the assailant has been looking for now is probably not related to the computer hacking that was done ten years ago." In Marsh's mind, that scenario made the most sense. "And if that's the case, then it's not likely that Geoff Colter is involved in his son's death."

Noel held up a hand. "I'm not sure about that. For all we know, father and son have gotten together and gone back to their old ways. They may have done some new hacking that produced this new mystery code."

"Yeah, okay." He couldn't argue that one. When Stacy returned, he ended the meeting. Riding together, they took the elevator back down to the lobby.

As they walked outside, Jackson stayed to Stacy's left. Marsh was on her right, with Noel Harrington on his other side. They stood for a moment outside the building. Call him paranoid, but Marsh didn't want Noel to see them leaving the area.

"Where are you parked?" Marsh asked Noel.

"On the street." Noel gestured to a black SUV. Jackson frowned, and walked toward it, angling to the side to see the license plate.

When Jackson turned back, he shook his head, indicating the license plate wasn't a match for the 840 number. Just then, another black SUV rolled toward them. When the driver's side window began to lower, Marsh anticipated a weapon and reacted instinctively.

He slammed the computer case into Noel with enough force to send the guy reeling into the black SUV. Then he turned toward Stacy, lifting her off the ground to get her back inside the building.

Jackson was hot on their heels. As Marsh led Stacy through the building to the rear exit and the parking lot where he'd left his SUV, he silently vowed not to trust anyone but his fellow rangers from this point forward.

# EIGHT

For the second time in an hour, Stacy followed Marsh through the back door of a building. Jackson was right behind her. An alarm sounded when they pushed past, but Marsh and Jackson ignored the noise. The men kept her sandwiched between them as they rushed toward the SUV parked in the rear lot.

Once she and Marsh were seated, Jackson stepped back and gestured for them to go. She wasn't sure where he'd parked, but Marsh didn't hesitate. Again, he jumped the curb to get away. She was used to the rocking of the SUV by now and simply hung on to the armrest to keep herself upright.

"Harrington isn't going to be happy," she finally said when the state building was well behind them. "Why did you slam him into the road?"

"Why was there a black SUV outside the state office building, which happens to be our meeting location?" Marsh shook his head in disgust. "I don't know what's going on, but when I saw the driver's side window go down, I feared the worst."

"I get that." She had been caught off guard at how effortlessly Marsh had lifted her off her feet to get her to safety. "But he may be badly hurt."

He shot her a quick glance. "I'll feel guilty about that if he's an innocent bystander. At this point I'm having a hard time trusting anyone other than Jackson, your brother, Sam and our boss."

Considering how little she knew about the man she'd married, she understood his perspective. "I get where you're coming from. It's just hard to see how Noel Harrington could be involved. He tried to get Damien into protective custody ten years ago. I highly doubt he's been working with the bad guys all this time."

Marsh frowned. "That's a good point. But the way we keep being found is driving me nuts."

"Maybe the bad guys anticipated you would head back to the state office building. That is your headquarters, after all. And you said yourself, they probably know you're a Texas Ranger."

"Possibly." His gaze lingered on the rearview mirror. "I don't see anyone behind us now, thankfully. As soon as we're outside the city, we need to find a safe house for you."

"Do the rangers have safe houses?" This was the first she'd heard of such a thing.

"Not like the US Marshals Service does." He grimaced, then pulled his phone from his pocket. "Do me a favor and call Jackson. He was going to ask Sam to find us a place to stay."

"I remember." She took the phone and found the most recent number. Jackson picked up on the first ring.

"Marsh?" His voice sounded tense as if expecting bad news.

"No, it's Stacy. We're fine. Marsh wants to know if Sam found us a place to stay."

"Oh yeah, I forgot to provide the information to Marsh before we left. Hang on a minute." There was a long moment of silence. "Sam found a place not far from Lake Travis. It's not right on the water, but the property is wooded and isolated."

"Okay, text me the address." She glanced at Marsh. "Are you familiar with Lake Travis?"

"No, but I've heard about it. It's a nice spot for water sports." Marsh arched a brow. "Sam found a rental home there?"

"Yes." She turned back to Jackson on the phone. "Can you meet us at the property?"

"That's the plan," Jackson agreed. "Did the address come through?"

She checked the text messages. "It did. We'll head that way now. See you there."

"Okay, oh, and let Marsh know that I've already heard from Harrington. He is not happy."

She winced. "I guess I can't blame him."

"I can," Marsh muttered, obviously able to hear a portion of the conversation. She held the phone between them so he could listen in.

"The only good news for us is that the black SUV sped away and disappeared around the corner after the incident," Jackson continued. "Noel understands why Marsh was concerned, clearly the bad guys had shown up outside the office building, but he didn't appreciate being used as a distraction."

"Why not? Isn't that part of his job description? The

same way it's ours?" Marsh demanded. "He's put his life on the line before, and this isn't any different."

"Hey, I'm on your side," Jackson said. "And I reiterated to Noel that protecting Stacy was our primary mission. He reluctantly agreed."

Stacy felt bad about dragging everyone around her into danger. "The sooner I find the code, the better."

"That should help," Marsh said. "But we still need to figure out who these guys are. And so far, all we have is the partial license plate. We need to dig into who the SUV may belong to."

"I asked Nina to assist with that," Jackson said. "She's sending a list of vehicles and their registered owners to me as soon as she has it. Oh, and Nina did confirm that Dan Copland, aka Damien had worked for Tech Guard for five years."

"Good to know the list of plate registrants is on the way." Marsh glanced at her, then asked, "What kind of place did Sam rent for us?"

"A small two-bedroom, two-bathroom home. As I told Stacy, it's not right on the lake, but there are plenty of woods surrounding the house, at least according to the photos Sam sent."

"Being inside a house that's surrounded by trees could work against us as far as someone sneaking up on the place." Marsh frowned. "Although the perps would have to leave their vehicle to head out on foot to get close. And so far, they seem more apt to try shooting from afar."

"If you want something different, I'm open to suggestions," Jackson said.

Stacy watched as Marsh thought for a moment. Then he sighed. "I say we use the house nestled in the trees. If we can get to the property without being tracked or seen, then we should be safe there. Oh, and that means not using your GPS via your car or phone."

"Got it. I'll meet you there." Jackson disconnected from the call.

Stacy dropped the phone in the center console cup-holder. "Since Nina was able to put a redirect on the ISP address of my computer, I'm sure we'll be fine. We have to assume these guys are computer savvy enough to have tracked the computer over the past few days."

Marsh nodded slowly. "If that's true, they may have pinged your computer at the state office building prior to Nina doing the redirect. Maybe that's why the black SUV showed up when it did."

She considered that and decided he was probably right. "I guess we should be looking for some sort of computer code. That must be what Damien stole."

"I still think it could be a bank account or a code to a lockbox or something else." Marsh turned to head west toward Lake Travis. "The bottom line has to be cold, hard cash."

"I keep going back to how Damien was fired from his job at Tech Guard." The baby kicked, distracting her. Without thinking, she grabbed Marsh's hand and placed it over her stomach. "Feel that?"

"Wow." His eyes widened in amazement. "She really is going to be a karate instructor one day."

"Soccer player first. Then maybe karate." She held his hand for a long moment, but her daughter's kicking stopped, so she released it. She felt herself flush over her need to share the experience with Marsh.

The way she had anticipated sharing every part of her pregnancy with her husband.

Enough. She wasn't going to keep dwelling on the man who'd lied to her. Damien was gone. She needed to move forward with her life.

She risked a glance at Marsh from beneath her lashes. His handsome profile, chiseled chin and warm brown eyes made her long for something more. But that was ridiculous. She wasn't interested in getting married again.

And there was no reason on earth Marsh would be interested in her in that way. Not only was she Tucker's younger sister, but she was pregnant.

No man in his right mind would volunteer to step into a ready-made family.

But knowing that in her head didn't mean her heart was listening.

Following the signs for Lake Travis, Marsh tried to figure out exactly where their rental property was located. He'd come to depend on GPS and map applications to lead them in the correct direction.

But he had no intention of using either of those methods now. Staying off grid meant doing things the old-fashioned way.

"Tell me the street name again?" He glanced at Stacy, who appeared lost in thought. "Stacy? Are you okay?"

"Huh? Oh, yes." She flushed. "Sorry. The street name?" She lifted the phone and recited the address. "It's 1420 Birch Tree Road. How are we going to find this place if you've never been here before?"

He chuckled. "I've heard of Lake Travis and have

driven past the area. I'm just hoping to figure it out once we get closer."

"We can always stop to ask for directions," Stacy suggested. "Do they still sell maps in gas stations?"

"Not street maps, but it's a good idea to check for tourist maps that might be available." He shot her a look of admiration. "Thanks for the suggestion."

She flushed again, and he couldn't help thinking how beautiful she was. The way she'd grabbed his hand to share the baby's kicks had deeply touched him. He hated the thought of her going through the rest of her pregnancy and delivery alone.

Well, she wouldn't be alone. She had Tuck and his wife Leanne who would be there for her.

She didn't need or likely want him to be involved. They might be friends, but that sort of connection didn't extend to the delivery room.

Giving himself a mental shake, he focused on the task at hand. They desperately needed this rental property to be a safe haven for Stacy.

Running from one motel to the next, or one restaurant to another, was getting old. What if all this stress caused her to deliver the baby early?

He kept a keen eye on the road behind them. But once they reached the stretch of highway that took them well outside the Austin city limits, he relaxed. Being away from the congested traffic was a relief. Yet he stayed alert, watching the rearview mirror for anything suspicious.

Like another black SUV.

When they were within five miles from Lake Travis, he pulled into the driveway of a gas station. They'd need food and other supplies for the rental house, as room service wasn't an option. Or nearby restaurants.

"Give me a few minutes to fill the gas tank," he said when she moved to get out of the car. "We'll head inside together."

"Okay." She sat back in her seat.

To his surprise, Jackson pulled in beside him. His buddy grinned. "Great minds."

"Yeah." He was glad to have Jackson there for backup to the monumental task of keeping Stacy safe.

When their respective gas tanks were full, he went around to open Stacy's door. She smiled at the newcomer. "Hi, Jackson. You made good time."

"So did you." Jackson turned to Marsh. "I stayed behind you to make sure you weren't followed. I think we're in the clear."

"Good, thanks for doing that." Marsh was impressed he hadn't noticed Jackson behind him. For the first time in eons, he was beginning to believe they were safe out here. "Let's grab some groceries and check out the tourist maps."

"Tourist maps?" Jackson looked confused. "Oh, you mean to see if we can locate the rental house. Sam mentioned we should take Hickory Lane to Birch Tree Road. From there, I'm not sure, but I figure the property will be well marked."

Marsh made sure Stacy was between them as they headed inside. She turned toward the grocery aisle while he stopped near the maps. There were several of Lake Travis, including one of hiking trails. A quick scan didn't reveal Hickory Lane or Birch Tree Road, but there was a wooded area off to one side of the trail. He made a note of the street names there before tucking the maps into his pocket.

Fifteen minutes later, when it seemed they had enough food to feed an army, he and Jackson carried the bags to their cars.

"You'll stay behind us?" Marsh asked Jackson.

"Yep. All the way." Jackson flashed a cheeky smile. "Try not to get lost."

Marsh rolled his eyes and slid behind the wheel. He handed Stacy the maps. "Help keep me on track."

"Gotcha."

Finding the rental property wasn't as difficult as he'd anticipated, thanks to the map of the hiking trails. He located Willow Bend, then happened upon Hickory Lane.

The driveway to their rental was so covered with trees that he missed it and had to turn back around. The house was small but nice, at least on the outside. He parked in front of the garage. "Stay here, while I access the house."

Stacy yawned and nodded. "Okay."

Jackson pulled in as he was entering the code. Opening the front door, he was greeted by a modern interior. He headed over to the attached garage and opened its door.

"Pull in," he told Jackson as he helped Stacy exit the vehicle. "Go on inside. We'll bring the groceries."

He and Jackson carried everything inside. Marsh drove into the second bay, then closed the garage door behind them. Having both cars hidden away inside the attached garage brought another wave of relief. The only way the bad guys could find them is if they discovered the address. Just driving by to search for them wasn't going to cut it.

Stacy was putting the groceries away. Marsh gently

nudged her aside. "I'll take care of this. Why don't you start working on the computer?"

"Okay." She flashed him a grateful look. "I'll try to be quick. I'm sure you'll need to look up some stuff on the laptop as well."

"I'll check in with Nina," Jackson said. "I had hoped to have that list of license plates by now."

Marsh glanced at his watch. The hour was still a bit early for dinner, but they'd been through a lot over the past few hours. He pulled out a cluster of grapes and set them in a bowl. Then he placed the bowl on the table. "In case you need to snack," he said.

"Thanks." She didn't take her gaze off the screen. He finished with the groceries, then crossed over to join her at the table.

"Can I help?" he asked.

"Not really." She grimaced. "I'm not one hundred percent sure what I'm looking for."

"Hey, Nina just sent me the list of registrations that match the partial license plate." Jackson dropped into the third chair at the table. "We need to check them out, see if anyone looks suspicious."

"We should have gotten a second laptop," Marsh muttered.

"Go ahead and use this one." Stacy pushed the computer toward Jackson.

She was so quiet, Marsh grew concerned. "Is something wrong?"

She broke off a sprig of grapes. "Nothing really, it's just hard coming to grips with the fact I married a criminal."

Marsh exchanged a quick look with Jackson. "You couldn't have known."

She lifted a shoulder and popped a grape in her mouth. "Doesn't change the fact that Damien stole a code. One I'm sure he planned to sell on the black market." She frowned. "Whatever it is."

"We'll figure it out." Marsh spoke with more confidence than he felt.

"You don't think any of this is related to the original crime?" Jackson asked. "Accessing the Department of Defense database?"

"Who knows?" Stacy looked glum. "But as Noel Harrington pointed out, that information is likely too old to be of any value these days. He also said the military had mitigated the damage. No, the more I think about it, the more I believe Damien must have gone back to his hacking ways and found something new to steal."

"I tend to agree." Marsh eyed Stacy. "You didn't know anything about his hacking skills?"

"No." She ate another grape. "But some of the things he said make more sense now. He told me that his job at Tech Guard was to attempt to breach their security systems, and by doing that, they could make them stronger."

"Sounds like the perfect job for him," Marsh murmured. "Considering he had firsthand experience in cracking through defense systems."

"I'd like to believe Damien was on the straight and narrow when we met. That he didn't go back to hacking until recently." Her blue eyes reflected anguish. "But really, he could have been hacking the entire time."

He ached to reassure her. But there was no way to

know what Dan aka Damien had done. "We'll know more once we find the code."

"I hope so." She pushed the grapes away as if talking about Damien was messing with her appetite.

His, too, to be honest.

Jackson looked up from the computer screen. "Okay, Nina has sent the list of registered cars that match the partial plate and the general make and model of a black SUV. There are only fourteen, which is interesting. I had expected a lot more."

"Can I take a look?" Marsh leaned forward to see the screen.

Jackson turned the laptop toward him. Scanning the names, it didn't take long to narrow the list of fourteen down to three highly probable options.

"I say we start with these." He tapped the screen to indicate the three vehicles in question. "The registrants are males in the same age range as the knife guy. If none of these pan out we can move on to the others. We'll use the laptop to dig into their backgrounds. Maybe one of them will have a criminal record."

"Okay." Jackson glanced at him. "But having a criminal record doesn't mean much. Could be our guy has created a fake identity for himself like…" His voice trailed off as Stacy looked up.

"Like Damien," she finished. "I agree that's a possibility, but I also think we should prioritize anyone with a criminal record."

Marsh dragged the computer toward him and began to input the information. The first guy on the list was clean, and when he did a routine search, the website of a law office popped up. The picture on both the driver's license and the website matched.

He moved on to the second name. Upon entering that name in the database, he got a hit. "Hey, this Alex Kowalski guy has been arrested for illegally selling handguns. He was let out a year ago and just finished probation."

"Bingo," Jackson murmured. "It's not a stretch to go from illegally selling guns to illegally using them."

"Exactly." He eyed the photograph of Alex Kowalski, then turned the computer to show Stacy.

She leaned forward, then went pale. "That's him." Her voice was shaky, but her gaze resolute. "That's the guy who held me at knifepoint."

It was their first real break in the case. And as Marsh used his phone to call the local cops to issue a BOLO (Be On the Lookout), he prayed that they'd find Alex Kowalski very soon.

Before he could make another attempt to get to Stacy.

# NINE

Stacy found it difficult to look away from the face of Alex Kowalski, the man who'd held her at knifepoint. He didn't look nearly as menacing on the screen as he had in real life when he'd grabbed her. If she'd have passed him on the street, she wouldn't have given him a second thought.

As she stared at his features, she wondered if Alex was the man who'd killed Damien. Was it possible this Alex worked for someone else? He'd claimed the code was stolen but hadn't indicated it was taken from him directly. She'd assumed he was the owner or originator of the code. A man who sold guns illegally and attacked a woman at knifepoint didn't seem the type to understand computer codes, though. He seemed to be more a thug than a tech wiz.

She felt certain Kowalski was working for someone else. Maybe even someone at Tech Guard. Because the more she thought about the series of events that had started with Damien losing his job, then getting murdered, she believed the code likely belonged to someone at the company.

"Okay, the Austin Police Department has issued a

BOLO for Kowalski's vehicle." Marsh gave her a nod. "Based on your identifying him as your attacker, we'll arrest him for aggravated assault with a deadly weapon."

"That's good news." Her baby kicked and somersaulted in her womb, reminding her of how close she and her daughter had come to being killed. She splayed her hands over her abdomen, knowing she would absolutely testify against Kowalski if needed to.

Anything to get him off the street.

"I've turned my regular phone off so that we can't be tracked here," Jackson said. "But at some point, we need to reach out to Noel Harrington. He should know about Kowalski."

"I don't know." Marsh scowled. "I still don't know that I trust the guy."

Stacy understood Marsh's concern. "But why would Noel be involved with the stolen code? He's been a US Marshal for more than ten years. It doesn't make sense that he'd suddenly turn bad."

"Stacy's right," Jackson said. "For Harrington to be dirty, he would have had to track Damien down to his new identity of Dan Copeland, then work with him to steal the code. That doesn't make any sense."

Marsh stood and paced the room. "Okay, you're right. I'm probably overreacting to how we've been found so easily. Kowalski must be smart when it comes to tracking and figuring out our next moves better than I've given him credit for."

"I understand." She managed a weak smile. "This has been an eventful day."

"And it's not over yet." Marsh moved to the window, staring out at the woods surrounding them before glancing back at her. "We're safe here, though. I don't see how Kowalski or anyone he's working with can find us here."

Jackson rose to his feet. "I may head back to Austin long enough to obtain a new laptop and to fill Owens in on what's been happening."

"Owens?" She frowned. Then remembered that was the name of Tucker's boss. "Oh, right, you guys report to John Owens."

"Yeah." Marsh scrubbed his hands over his face. "I'd appreciate your help with both of those things. Ask our boss for more resources while you're at it. I would like to have guys posted outside the rental house."

"I'll try," Jackson said. "But that may only draw attention to the place."

"See what the boss thinks. Oh, and you may as well fill Harrington in on what we know so far," Marsh added. "And please make sure you're not followed."

"Absolutely," Jackson promised. He glanced at her, then back to Marsh. "I'll be back within one to two hours at the most. Sam chose a nice spot to rent a house. We're only thirty miles outside of Austin."

"Be safe." Marsh walked Jackson to the door, then made sure it was locked. When he turned to face her, she couldn't help but catch her breath.

It wasn't just that Marsh was handsome, although he certainly was. Damien had been handsome, too. No, this simmering attraction was related to his steely determination to protect her. To keep her and her unborn daughter safe.

He had more integrity in his baby toe than her husband had possessed in his entire body.

Knowing her hormones were running amok, she forced

herself to turn away and reach for the laptop. "I still think Damien must have hidden the code somewhere within my computer programs. He'd want it both protected from being found but close at hand for whenever he needed to retrieve it."

"You'll find it." Marsh crossed the room to lightly cup her shoulders with his hands. It was all she could do not to turn and press her face into his chest. "But don't push yourself too hard, either. If you get tired, take a nap."

His tenderness was nearly her undoing. She blinked back the threat of tears and swallowed hard against the lump in her throat. "I'm fine."

"Just know I'm here if you need me." Marsh released her and stepped back. She instantly missed the warmth of his hands.

With a nod, since she didn't trust herself to speak, she turned her attention to the computer. She still had her email program to get through. And as she stared at her inbox, a sudden thought occurred to her.

She and Damien had exchanged several emails over time. Mostly related to mundane things, like making dinner plans or discussing bills that needed to be paid. They both worked full-time jobs, so it was often easier to shoot an email back and forth than to make a call.

Thankfully, she hadn't gone through her email to delete them. If Damien was going to hide a code, he may have simply found a way to email it to her.

Leaning forward, she hit a few keys to sort her email folder by sender, isolating those Damien had sent, then began to go through each one.

It was harder than she'd anticipated. Seeing their notes,

that had often ended with *I love you*, brought memories of their time together tumbling back.

While she knew now that the messages were shrouded in lies, at the time she'd thought his love was real.

As real as hers.

When she reached the message where they were arranging their schedules for the ultrasound, hot tears filled her eyes.

And this time, she couldn't hold them back.

She pushed up from the table and turned to seek an escape. Suddenly Marsh was there, pulling her into his arms and holding her close.

"Don't cry, please don't cry," he whispered, his voice low and agonized.

Ironically, his attempt to be sweet and reassuring only made her cry harder. Because Marsh was everything she wanted in a husband. A man who would love and cherish her while also being a wonderful father to her baby girl.

Yet she also knew that her dream would never become a reality. Her future was not entwined with his.

When this nightmare was over, she'd raise her daughter alone.

Marsh had never felt so helpless in his entire life. He didn't know what to do or to say to make Stacy feel better. He decided all he could do was to hold her close and be there for her.

After a few minutes, she lifted her head and pushed away. "I need to stop doing this," she muttered as she went into the kitchen for a paper towel. "I don't usually cry this much in one day."

"Hey, you're entitled to cry whenever you want." He

winced at his inane words. Of course she was riding an emotional roller coaster. She'd learned her husband lied, then she'd been targeted by gunfire more than once. He glanced around the room. "What can I do to help?" He spied the computer. "Should I go through your computer to find the code?"

"No. I'm more likely to spot something unusual than you are. Excuse me." She ducked into the powder room, returning a few minutes later. "I'm sorry."

"Don't apologize," he said firmly. "None of this is your fault, Stacy. I am willing to do whatever it takes to help you through this."

"I know, and that's the problem." She winced, then hastily added, "I appreciate your support, Marsh. Truly. It's just difficult to look back at my life before Damien's death knowing what I do now."

"You keep calling him Damien," he noted.

"Yeah." She tucked a strand of hair behind her ear. "Hoping to reinforce in my mind that Dan never existed."

He understood. Leaning toward the computer, he caught an email on the screen. He didn't take the time to read the contents of the message, but the Love Dan at the end was more than enough for him to understand what had happened.

Again, he tried to think of a way to make her feel better. "I'm sure your husband loved you. I don't think he'd have married you if he hadn't."

"Putting me and our baby in danger is a funny way of showing that." She waved a hand. "Whatever. His feelings for me aren't relevant any longer. I'll be fine. I know God has brought me along this troubled path for a reason. I'm glad the truth has come out."

He admired her strength and determination more than he could have thought possible. His heart ached for her. When he took a step toward her, his phone rang.

Recognizing Jackson's number, he quickly answered. "What happened?"

"Nothing's wrong," Jackson said quickly. "I'm at the state building now, reviewing the video tape of the black SUV. I was surprised to find that Harrington was still here. We had an interesting conversation about the black SUV and Alex Kowalski. He's still upset about how you smacked him, but hearing about Kowalski has smoothed things over. Noel is now convinced, as I am, that the missing code is related to something recent. Not the Colters hacking into the DOD database ten years ago."

"Yeah, I believe that, too." Marsh watched as Stacy made some herbal tea. "Stacy has been going through her emails from Damien but so far hasn't found anything."

"Noel has offered to help us with the case, but I assured him we had it under control." There was a brief pause before he continued. "He's going to keep searching for Geoff Colter, just in case the father and son did reunite at some point."

"That's probably a good idea," Marsh admitted. "For all we know, Geoff and Damien worked together to steal the code."

"Yep. Noel wants Colter badly. I think he's still angry over how Colter got away with hacking into the DOD database. If Geoff Colter is involved in this, we need Noel to find him."

Marsh wasn't sure how the US Marshals Service would manage that, but that was Noel Harrington's problem.

His was to keep Stacy safe while searching for the code. "Will Noel keep us updated?"

"Yes, and I promised to do the same." As if Jackson could see Marsh's frown, his buddy added, "I did not compromise your current location. I didn't tell Noel anything other than what we learned about Kowalski by tracking the partial license plate. Everything is fine. If we learn something Noel needs to know, I'll find a way to reach him."

Marsh relaxed. "Okay, thanks. Did you talk to Owens? Is he willing to provide additional resources?"

"I did, but he did not authorize another ranger to assist us." Jackson sighed. "Truth is, Sam has been assigned another case; Tuck is still with Leanne and Pops and I knew Stacy wouldn't want them to be left alone. Rather than drag another ranger into the mix, I figured we're better off to manage this between the two of us."

Marsh didn't like it but wasn't going to argue, either. Since he wasn't in a trusting mood, he silently acknowledged Jackson was probably right not to drag someone new into this. "Okay, I'm on board with that plan. Did you learn anything else?"

"Nothing helpful. The video of the black SUV doesn't reveal anything other than to validate the partial plate number that we have already associated with Alex Kowalski. Owens issued a statewide BOLO and an arrest warrant for the guy. At this point, all we can do is to wait and see if he gets picked up."

Waiting wasn't Marsh's strong suit. Suppressing his frustration, he asked, "Are you heading back soon?"

"Yes. That's why I called. Do you need me to pick up anything along the way? I already have a laptop from the office. Nina added the same protections that she used on Stacy's machine."

"Great. Hang on, I'll ask." He caught Stacy's gaze. "Do you need Jackson to bring anything? Any groceries we may have missed?"

"Not for me, but you guys may want coffee. I forgot to get some from the convenience store." Her eyes were still slightly red and puffy from her crying jag.

"We need coffee and filters for the coffee maker," he told Jackson. "Thanks."

"See you soon." Jackson ended the call.

Lowering his phone, he watched Stacy settle in behind the computer. Despite the emotional turmoil she'd been through, she seemed determined to do her part in solving this. When she glanced over at him questioningly, he realized he was staring.

"Sorry. I'm just thinking." He turned away, leaving her to it. She didn't need him hovering over her shoulder.

He moved from one window to the next, checking the view from each location. Even though there weren't many leaves on the trees, there were enough evergreens around the property that he couldn't see the homes located around them. Or the lake for that matter.

He liked the isolation for the most part, but it was also a little deceiving. Obviously, there were other people living in the area. This place was a nice vacation property, and under normal circumstances, he'd have enjoyed staying here.

Now he found himself thinking about ways to offer additional protection. An idea popped into his mind and he quickly called Jackson back. "Hey, pick up a few trail cams to cover the front and back doors."

"Good idea." Jackson didn't sound annoyed by the request. "Only two or do you want a few more?"

Was he being overly paranoid? Maybe. "Get four cameras. We'll use one to cover each side of the house."

"Will do." Jackson disconnected.

Marsh lowered his phone to find Stacy eyeing him curiously. "Trail cams?"

"Yes." He didn't want her to worry. "Probably overkill, but they'll provide another layer of protection. We can link them to the computer and they'll provide a warning if anyone comes too close."

"Sounds good." She went back to her work. After a few minutes, she turned back to face him. "I keep thinking about how Damien was fired from Tech Guard. The human resources representative I spoke to wouldn't give me any information about what happened. I understand there are privacy concerns, but Damien is dead."

Marsh crossed over to sit beside her. "You're thinking Damien stole the code from them?"

"I think the timing is suspicious. Two weeks after he's fired, he gets murdered?" She tapped the screen. "Check out the employees on their website."

He leaned forward to see the picture. "That's Matt Wade. You mentioned he was a friend of Dan's."

"Yes, and this guy here—" she tapped another photo "—is Frank Gingras. He's the director of operations, and if I remember correctly, Matt and Dan both reported to him. I recognize him from when I interviewed for a position there." Her blue eyes settled on his. "I think I should call Frank or Matt and tell them I found a folder on a laptop from our home that contains files that may belong to their company."

He nodded in admiration. "If they're aware of the missing code, they'll jump on the chance to meet with you and to retrieve the file."

"Exactly." She smiled. "And if so, we have reason to believe that someone from Tech Guard is responsible for hiring Alex Kowalski."

"The only problem with this plan is putting you in danger." Marsh frowned as he drummed his fingers on the table. "I don't want to leave the safety of this rental house."

"I understand, but we can't just sit here and wait for Alex Kowalski to be arrested." She reached over to rest her hand on his arm. "Please, Marsh. For this to work, I have to be there. It's more believable if I'm the one who calls to explain what I've found. I can even pretend that I don't want the police involved because I don't want to ruin Dan's good name." The light in her eyes dimmed. "Even though the truth is I don't care about protecting my late husband. Only my baby."

"Okay." He hoped he wouldn't regret going along with this. But he could see how this ploy could work. "Go ahead and make the call."

"I'll start with Matt Wade," she said. "If he doesn't seem interested or doesn't know what I'm talking about, I'll go up the chain to Frank."

"Use my phone, but try to make the call brief." He wasn't sure if the computer company could track his disposable cell phone or not. "Don't go into a lot of detail now."

She nodded and took the phone. Less than a minute later, he could tell there was no answer, so she left a message. "Hi, Matt, it's Stacy Copeland. I found a file on the computer that I shared with Dan that may belong to Tech Guard. Call me if you think it's important." She lowered the phone. "I should have anticipated he wouldn't answer a call from an unknown number."

"That's okay, you worded that perfectly." He grinned. "I bet he calls back—"

The phone rang before he could finish his sentence. She scooped it up, but then took a calming breath before answering. "Hello?" After a pause, she said, "Yes, I'm looking at the folder now. You think it's important? Okay, then I'll be happy to show you what I found. No, I can't email it. The file seems rather large."

"Set up the meeting for four thirty this afternoon," Marsh whispered.

She nodded. "I can meet you at four thirty if that works. Oh, sure, I know the Mexican restaurant near your office building. It's called La Fuentes, right? Okay, see you then." She ended the call and handed him the phone. "I hope that was short enough."

"It was. Now I'll arrange for Jackson to head to the restaurant so he can be in a position to watch for Wade to arrive." Marsh quickly called his buddy. Jackson didn't sound upset by the new plan and agreed to head over to La Fuentes.

"Matt sounded casually interested in the file," she said when Marsh had finished making the arrangements. "But I think the fact that he called back so quickly means he knows something about the missing code." She grimaced. "I should have considered doing this earlier."

"Hey, we've been busy dodging bullets." Marsh knew they might be onto something. The only downside to the plan was that they had to drive all the way back to San

Antonio. Good thing he'd asked for extra time. "Do you think we should bring Noel Harrington into this?"

"I don't think that's necessary." She rose to her feet. "We better go in case we run into traffic along the way."

He nodded and headed for the door. Taking Stacy to this meeting with Matt Wade was risky. But if the guy was involved, then they'd be one step closer to ending this nightmare for Stacy once and for all.

And he wanted that for her more than anything else in the world. She deserved that much.

# TEN

Stacy twisted her hands in her lap as Marsh headed down the driveway. When he reached the road, she had to resist the urge to look back at the rental house, the first place she'd felt safe in what seemed like forever.

Biting her lip, she reminded herself this meeting with Matt Wade had been her idea. And she wasn't that worried about something going wrong. She knew Marsh and Jackson would sacrifice themselves to protect her.

Yet she felt a little sick to her stomach knowing that she was putting two of her brother's closest friends in danger. She couldn't bear the thought of anything happening to Marsh or Jackson.

Especially Marsh.

"Jackson has a computer from the office." Marsh gestured to the laptop at her feet. "Push that beneath the seat for now. I don't want to risk losing the one item that may contain the mystery code."

"Okay." She awkwardly bent to shove the computer beneath her seat. "I'm glad Jackson will be in the restaurant as a backup."

"I'll be there, too." Marsh shot her a quick glance. "Don't even think about trying to meet with this guy alone. If you don't want Matt to know I'm a ranger, that's fine. You can pretend I'm your boyfriend."

She turned her strangled laugh into a cough. Just the idea of Marsh being her boyfriend was ludicrous. Yet at the same time, a warmth crept into her cheeks. Getting married again wasn't part of her plan, but if she did decide to go that route, she'd pick someone like Marsh.

Someone who would give her the kind of marriage her brother Tucker had with Leanne. A deep and abiding love that was not based on lies.

"Stacy?" Marsh prompted. "I'm going with you, okay?"

"Yes, that's fine. I'll simply tell him you're an old friend." She smiled teasingly. "Emphasis on old."

"That works for me." Marsh didn't laugh at her weak attempt at humor. He wasn't that much older than her, probably only five to six years. His expression remained tense as he alternated between watching their rearview mirror and driving. She reached out to put a hand on his arm.

"We'll be fine. If Matt wants the code, then he'll make a play for the computer not me."

"I know." This time he smiled. "I like the fact that he picked a public place. He probably thinks you'll hand over the computer without a problem."

"Exactly. And he's right about that. I wouldn't do anything to endanger my baby." She dropped her hand and shifted in her seat. The baby was moving around a lot, which was a good thing. But sometimes her daughter's foot got wedged up against her rib cage. Maybe Marsh was right about her baby becoming a karate instructor. The more she thought about it, the more she wished she'd taken more self-defense classes along the way. Sure,

Tucker had taught her a few things, including how to shoot a gun, but she hadn't realized how vulnerable she was until Alex Kowalski grabbed her from behind and held a knife at her throat.

Once this was over, she hoped and prayed her daughter would grow up feeling safe, secure and loved. They wouldn't be rich, but she would lean on God to support her through being a single parent.

To raise this precious child to become a capable, confident and caring adult.

When Marsh's phone rang, she startled badly.

"I'm sure it's Jackson." Marsh had noticed her inadvertent response. He handed her the phone. "Go ahead and talk to him while I concentrate on driving."

"Hi, Jackson." She willed her racing heart to return to normal. "Are you at La Fuentes already?"

"No, I'm still heading toward San Antonio. Let Marsh know that I picked up extra disposable phones in addition to the trail cameras. That way we can ditch the ones you're using now in case Matt Wade somehow gets away."

"I'll tell him." She quickly relayed the information to Marsh.

"Ask Jackson to have Nina run Matt Wade's background for us," Marsh said. "I'd like to know how he and Damien hooked up."

"Jackson? Ask Nina to do a deep dive into Matt Wade. Thanks." She lowered the phone. "I can tell you what I was told although I have no way of knowing if any of it is true. According to Damien, he met Matt Wade at a gaming convention. Apparently, the gaming community is pretty tight. They hit it off, especially since they were in similar careers."

"And that's when Matt agreed to give Damien a reference for his job at Tech Guard?" Marsh asked.

"Yes. Matt vouched for Damien, and his boss, Frank, hired him on the spot." She frowned, thinking back. "If Damien was telling me the truth, he and Matt worked in the same department but were responsible for different security projects. They were colleagues who both reported to Frank."

"Okay, so it could be that Matt didn't find out right away that Damien stole the code." Marsh's tone was thoughtful.

"Maybe, but he obviously knows now." She grimaced. "Maybe this is more about corporate espionage. It could be that Tech Guard has some key program that other tech companies would love to have for their systems."

"And, what, Damien planned to sell the code to the highest bidder?" Marsh frowned. "I'm not sure about that. If the company had lost the code, they wouldn't send a hired thug to threaten you with a knife to get it back."

"That's true." A chill snaked down her spine. Alex Kowalski, the knife guy, had said he wanted the code Damien had stolen. She'd assumed the code had been stolen from Kowalski, but maybe he'd meant that Damien had stolen it for him. She swallowed hard and added, "Unless the person he was going to sell it to paid Damian the money but never got the product? That would explain why he believes he's the rightful owner of the code."

"Could be." Marsh drove in silence for several long minutes. The traffic wasn't bad, so she anticipated they'd reach the restaurant in plenty of time. "Whatever happened with Tech Guard and the missing code, we'll know more after speaking to Matt Wade."

"I hope so." A wide yawn caught her off guard. Riding in the car made her feel sleepy. She blinked her eyes to stay awake.

"Relax, we'll be there in less than an hour." The way Marsh was so in tune to her emotions was uncanny. She glanced at him, then realized he was right. There was nothing she could do now, except to wait for them to get to the restaurant.

And to pray. She leaned her head back, closed her eyes and silently asked God to keep them safe in His care.

As the SUV ate up the miles, Marsh battled second thoughts about the wisdom of taking Stacy to this meeting. Maybe he could convince Jackson to stay in the SUV with her while he took the laptop to Matt Wade.

Glancing over at Stacy, he smiled when he realized she'd fallen asleep. Her position didn't look all that comfortable, her head resting against the passenger side window, but her serene expression was reassuring.

His heart ached for her. He hated that she was in danger through no fault of her own and while being pregnant. He wanted to wrap her in bulletproof material until they had Alex Kowalski—and whoever else was involved— behind bars.

His phone rang and he answered quickly, hoping the noise hadn't disturbed her sleep. "Yeah?" He kept his voice a low whisper.

"Hey, I'm at the restaurant," Jackson said. "The place is fairly busy, but I was able to snag a table in the corner that overlooks most of the dining area."

"Okay." Marsh glanced at Stacy, who hadn't roused

at the sound of the phone. "Anything stand out as suspicious?"

"Not yet," Jackson drawled. "I plan to order an early dinner to blend in with the others. Oh and the work laptop is in my SUV. You'll want to grab that to use for the meeting so we can protect Stacy's device."

"Yeah, thanks. Any word on Matt Wade?"

"I haven't heard back, but Nina is working on it." The way Jackson said Nina's name in a softer tone gave him pause. Did Jackson have more than a passing interest in their tech expert? "She's amazing."

"Agree." Marsh hid a smile. Oh yeah, Jackson was interested all right. And Marsh could relate. He glanced again at Stacy. If she wasn't reeling from a man who'd lied to her, he'd be in the same boat as Jackson. But he knew Tucker would have a fit if he expressed interest in his baby sister. Shoving that thought aside, he told himself to stay focused on the issue at hand. "See you soon."

Thirty minutes later, he exited the interstate and scoped out the restaurant. He'd noticed Jackson's rental in the back row of the parking lot and chose a space a few stalls down. Marsh didn't like making Stacy walk so far in her condition, but it was easier to get away out the back of the restaurant if necessary, as evidenced by their recent escape from the Coffee Corner Café and then again at the state building. He could only pray that wouldn't be required this time around.

"Stacy?" He kept the car running as he touched her arm. "We're here."

"Hmm?" She opened her eyes, blinked and then turned to look at him. "What? Really? I slept the whole time?"

"Most of the time," he corrected. "And I'm glad you were able to get some rest."

She tunneled her fingers through her hair, her cheeks flushed. "Well, thanks." Sweeping a glance over the parking lot, she frowned. "What's the plan?"

"Sit tight while I grab the laptop from Jackson's SUV, then touch base with him." He pushed out of the car, strode to the SUV and found the laptop tucked under the front seat. He carried it back to Stacy. "Hold on to this, will you?"

"Sure." She set it across her knees.

He quickly called his buddy. "Jackson? We're in the parking lot. What's happening?"

"Hey." Jackson's voice was subdued. "Our target just walked in, but he looks nervous."

Marsh's stomach knotted. "Nervous how?"

"Pacing back and forth. Hasn't agreed to sit at a table yet. Glancing at his watch frequently."

"He's early," Marsh said.

"So are we. It could be he's waiting for someone else to show up?"

"Like someone to back him up?" Marsh scowled, not liking that idea. "If someone else shows up, we're out of here."

"Roger that," Jackson murmured. "For now, I say hold tight. Let's give him a few minutes to let this play out. See if he's got another plan up his sleeve."

"Yeah, okay. Call me back in a few." Marsh lowered the phone and looked at Stacy. "Matt Wade is inside, but Jackson said he looks nervous."

"I'm nervous, too." She frowned, eyeing the rear door of the restaurant. He'd backed into the parking space to facilitate a quick escape. "You're thinking we should just go back to the rental house at Lake Travis?"

"I don't know." He wanted to be inside the restaurant to watch Matt Wade for himself. Not that he didn't trust Jackson's judgment, because he did. He couldn't stand the thought of leading Stacy into a potential trap. "What I'd really like is to take Matt Wade into custody if he's involved. It's figuring that part out that's the problem."

"We'll need to go inside eventually," Stacy said with a shrug. "Maybe once he sees me, he'll make his move."

"Yeah, that's what I'm afraid of." He eyed his watch. It was four fifteen. He reached for the phone to call Jackson again. "Anything new?"

"Subject has finally taken a seat at a table with a direct line of sight to the main entrance," Jackson's tone was still quiet. "I think you and Stacy should come in through the side entrance, the one leading in from the outside patio. Nobody is sitting out there in February, so the door may be locked. I'll head that way to let you in."

"I like that idea." Going into the restaurant through the patio would give them a slight advantage. "We'll be there in a minute."

"Understood." Jackson ended the call.

"Okay, we're heading to that side patio." Marsh slid out from behind the wheel then ran around to get her door. Stacy wiggled out of the seat, then reached for the decoy laptop. "I'm ready."

"Great. Stay close to me, okay?" He slid his arm around her waist as they moved toward the side of the building. He had to smile when he noticed the door was ajar. He reached for the handle and pulled it open. Jackson, who must have propped it open for them, was already back inside the restaurant.

Marsh stepped inside, drawing Stacy in beside him. Then he closed the door and edged further into the space. The restaurant had basically two main dining areas. One was closer to the front door and was obviously where customers were seated first. The rear space was used more as overflow during busy times.

Four thirty in the afternoon was too late for lunch and on the early side for dinner. There weren't any customers sitting in the back section of the restaurant, which was nice. He moved closer to the arched opening that led to the front-facing dining room and scanned the tables for Wade.

He spotted Jackson first, then caught a glimpse of a man seated at a table facing the door. Without seeing the guy's face, it was difficult to ascertain his identity.

But then he noticed the man fidgeting in his seat and knew he'd found Matt Wade.

"Okay, do you see him?" He spoke to Stacy in a low voice. "He's sitting three tables ahead of us and one over to the right."

"I see him." Stacy had the laptop tucked under her arm. She gave him a quick glance and nodded. "I'm ready."

He wanted to give her a hug and a kiss but made do with a reassuring smile. He stepped forward, keeping his arm firmly around Stacy's waist. They approached Matt along the right side, because Marsh had noticed the guy's right hand was his dominant one.

And if they had to react quickly to a threat, Marsh would have the advantage of being on his strong side.

Matt Wade was so engrossed in watching the front door for them that he didn't notice Marsh and Stacy coming up alongside him until they were parallel to the table. When Wade recognized Stacy, he looked surprised.

"Oh, uh, how did I miss you?" Wade's shaky tone betrayed his nervousness.

"Hi, Matt." Stacy's remarkably calm voice didn't seem to help Wade relax. If anything, the guy nearly fell out of his seat as he tried to stand. "Oh, please don't get up."

"Stacy, uh, who's this?" Matt Wade's gaze zeroed in on Marsh. "I thought you were coming alone?"

"This is Marsh, he's a friend of mine." Stacy moved toward the chair across from Wade. Marsh stayed to Wade's right.

"Is that the laptop where you found the folder?" Matt's gaze seemed glued to the laptop that Stacy still had tucked under her arm. To the guy's credit, he didn't lunge forward to grab it.

But Marsh sensed that he wanted to.

"Yes, but before I get to that, I was hoping you could help me understand something." Stacy dropped into the chair across from Wade, effectively keeping the laptop out of the guy's reach.

"Uh, sure." Matt frowned, clearly not happy with the delay. "What's up?"

"Why was Dan fired?" Stacy's question was a surprise to Marsh; she hadn't mentioned her plan to ask about her dead husband's career. Although now that she had, he thought it was brilliant.

"How should I know?" Matt's response came a little too quick.

"You were friends, Matt." Again, Stacy's reasonable tone made Marsh hide a smile. She didn't look the least bit nervous now, despite her claim to the contrary. "You helped Dan get that job. You must know why he was fired. Especially since it was only a couple of weeks later that he was mugged and killed."

Matt glanced at Marsh, as if realizing he was boxed in. "Look, I don't know exactly what happened. The rumor going around the company was that Dan took something that doesn't belong to him."

Like the code? Marsh kept his eyes trained on Wade. The guy hadn't relaxed at all since they'd come up to his table. Quite the opposite. Wade was more jittery and anxious than ever.

"You didn't talk to Dan after he was let go?" Stacy persisted. "I would think Dan would confide in you."

"Why didn't Dan confide in you?" Matt shot back.

Rather than responding to his comment, Stacy pulled the laptop out from under her arm and set it on the table. Wade's gaze immediately went to the laptop. "Shall I show you the strange file?" she asked.

"No. I'll take it from here." When Wade reached for the laptop, Marsh grabbed his forearm.

"Not so fast." He tightened his grip in warning, then released it. "Why don't you tell us what you think is on the device?"

"That wasn't part of the deal." Matt looked almost desperate now, his gaze darting between Stacy and Marsh. Then Marsh watched as the Tech Guard employee's right hand dip toward his pocket.

Did Wade have a gun? Marsh reached for the laptop. He brought it up and off the table and struck Wade in the face. The man let out a surprised wail, nearly falling backward out of his chair.

There was also a loud clatter as something hard hit the floor.

"Gun!" someone screamed. "He has a gun!"

Jackson rushed over to scoop up the weapon. "We're Texas rangers," Jackson said in a loud voice. "Everything is fine. There's no reason to panic."

Instantly, the screaming subsided. Marsh stood and wrenched Matt Wade to his feet, gripping his wrists and roughly clasping them behind the guy's back. "You were going to pull a gun on a pregnant woman?"

"I—I—" Wade stammered. "I need the laptop! Please just give me the laptop."

"And why would we do that?" Marsh asked.

Wade's face flushed. "Because it belongs to Tech Guard. Dan stole it."

"The laptop Dan used for work was taken the night he was mugged," Stacy said.

Wade's eyes widened. "I know that, but you said there was a program on this laptop that you thought was related to the company. I was told I had to get it back."

"Told by whom?" Marsh asked.

"I—I'm not sure." Wade was practically babbling now. "He didn't provide his name, just that I had to get the laptop back or risk being fired, too."

Marsh met Stacy's surprised gaze. This had not gone down at all the way he'd expected. Especially if Matt Wade was telling the truth about not knowing who ordered him to get the laptop back.

Even with Matt Wade in custody, they were no closer to getting out of this mess.

# ELEVEN

What in the world was going on? Stacy glowered at Matt, angry that he'd brought a gun to their meeting with the intent to threaten her with it. The other customers in the restaurant were gawking at them, and with good reason.

"You must know who called you." She held his gaze. "Someone within Tech Guard? Maybe your boss, Frank Gingras?"

"It didn't sound like Frank." Matt looked away and stared down at the floor. "But yeah, it was someone using a Tech Guard phone number."

"What was the number?" she asked. "There must have been a name associated with it. Your phones have caller ID built in, don't they?" The ones at her company did.

"Yeah, but the call came from an unidentified number." Matt sighed. "There are some offices that are used by staff who rotate from one place to the other. The call originated from one of those shared offices."

"What exactly did the caller say?" Marsh asked.

"He told me that it was my job to get Dan's laptop back. That I should call you to get the computer. And if I didn't, I would end up looking for a new job."

Stacy thought it was strange that he'd only be threatened with losing his job. Tech companies were always looking for new people. It was one of the fastest growing industries out there. It wasn't as if Matt couldn't secure another position. "Why would they fire you over a laptop?"

"How should I know?" Matt hunched his shoulders. "I thought it was strange that they would threaten me. Made me afraid that I'd end up like Dan, too."

"Wait a minute." She grabbed his arm. "Which is it? Fired or end up like Dan?"

Matt looked confused. "It's one and the same."

Shaking her head, she let him go and glanced at Marsh. "No, it's not. Dan is dead. He was murdered."

The color leeched from Matt's face. "I'm sure that's not what the guy meant."

"Isn't it?" She knew very well that it was. That Matt had been used as a pawn by the person who was really behind this. "Go back to what this guy told you. He actually said that you should get the laptop? The one that was taken during his mugging?"

"He said 'laptop,'" Matt repeated. "I tried to call you, but you never answered your phone. I must have left you five messages. I was shocked when you called me. And when you said you had a program on a computer you shared with Dan, I figured that was the one this guy was looking for. Especially if it had Tech Guard information on it. For all I knew, your computer was the important one."

Marsh released Matt's wrists and pushed him back into the chair. "You need to start at the beginning. Dan was fired two weeks before he was murdered. Did he tell you why he was let go?"

"Dan refused to take my calls." Matt didn't look as scared now, as if he finally understood they were trying to help him. "I was irritated, you know? I mean, I gave him a reference so that he could work at Tech Guard in the first place. We worked together for over five years, although not on the same projects. I wanted to know what happened, especially with the rumors going around that he stole something. But he wouldn't answer any of my calls or text messages."

Stacy frowned. "Dan hadn't confided in me, either. I didn't know he'd been let go until after his death."

"Wow." Matt appeared stunned at the news. "I can't imagine keeping something like that from my wife. Not that I'm married, but still."

That was the least of the lies Dan had told her, but she wasn't sure if that was something they should share with Matt. She glanced at Marsh.

"When did the guy from the unidentified Tech Guard number call you?" Marsh asked.

"Yesterday around nine thirty in the morning." Matt's voice was subdued. "I guess I assumed the guy worked at Tech Guard. But now that I think about it, he may not have been an employee."

"What makes you say that?" Stacy asked.

"I don't know. It's all very confusing." Matt raked his hands through his hair. "He asked me if I was Matt Wade, which he should have known, right? After I said yes, he told me that I needed to call Dan's widow, Stacy. That it was my job to get Dan Copeland's laptop back or I'd end up like him. Before I could ask him anything else, he disconnected from the call."

"Did you go to the office where the call was made?" Marsh asked.

"I thought about it," Matt admitted. "But then I got scared. I stayed in my office and pretended to work." He shot her a glance. "Why didn't you answer any of my calls?"

She arched a brow. "Because I'm in danger. That same person who called you has been threatening me."

Matt's gaze dropped to her pregnant belly, then darted away. He looked miserable, as if he didn't understand how he'd gotten to this point.

And really, no matter how upset she was with him for bringing a gun to their meeting, she understood Matt Wade was a victim in this, too.

Just like she was.

"Okay, we're going to take you in to be debriefed, and for your protection," Marsh said. "I don't think you should go back to Tech Guard until we understand what's going on."

Matt's expression bloomed with hope. "You'll keep me safe?"

"Yeah." Marsh turned to Jackson. "I'll need you to drive him to Austin. We can put him up in a motel there for a few days."

"Understood." Jackson stepped forward and grasped Matt Wade's arm. "Come with me."

Matt rose to his feet, then turned to face her. "I'm sorry, Stacy. I never would have hurt you."

She didn't entirely believe him but forced a reassuring smile. God expected her to practice forgiveness. And really, that included forgiving her late husband, too. "Take care, Matt."

"I don't want to die," Matt said as Jackson escorted him from the restaurant.

"I know." Jackson gave Marsh a nod. "I'll see you later."

"Yep." Both men were careful not to mention where they'd meet up. Stacy watched as Matt left, his head bowed in defeat.

"Why would they ask him to get the laptop?" She turned to face Marsh. "Why not do it themselves?"

"I think they assumed your guard would be down with him, as he was your husband's friend." Marsh reached for her hand. "Time for us to get out of here."

She nodded, not at all surprised when he led her back through the restaurant to the patio door they'd used to enter. When Marsh stood there for a moment, scanning the area outside, she understood he was worried that the mystery caller may be sitting close by, watching.

Only after a full five minutes, during which Jackson left with Matt Wade, did Marsh glance down at her. "Wait here. I'll bring the car over."

"Okay." She stepped back, giving him room to leave. A minute later, Marsh pulled up beside the building. Stacy darted out and jumped inside.

"Are you okay?" Marsh asked once they were back on the road. He was doing the now familiar maneuvers where he made frequent turns, heading in different directions before ending up on the interstate highway.

"Fine." She smoothed her hands over her belly. "I wasn't as scared as Matt Wade."

"Yeah. Wade was in way over his head." Marsh

frowned. "I hadn't seriously considered that Tech Guard was a key part of this."

She hadn't, either. "Their mission seems to include either getting the code or the laptop. Which is odd since they must know the laptop was stolen the day of Dan's murder. It's on the ATM video."

Marsh nodded thoughtfully. "I'm sure the ultimate goal is the code, which they have reason to believe is on the missing laptop."

A sudden thought hit hard. She grabbed Marsh's arm. "We're assuming the laptop was stolen the day of Dan's murder. But what if Dan hid it prior to that? What if the laptop is still out there somewhere?"

Marsh arched a brow. "You said a laptop was taken the day of the murder and that the robbery is on video. But you're right that the laptop may not have been the one with the code. But if that's the case, why not keep Damien alive long enough to know where the actual laptop was hidden?"

"They may have just assumed that laptop he had was the one they needed. And maybe it was. I'm just throwing ideas out there." She released Marsh's arm and stared out the window. She'd hoped that meeting with Matt would have told them more about what was going on.

But she felt more lost than ever about where to look for the mystery code.

Determined to avoid being followed, Marsh traveled north for several miles while keeping a keen eye on the rearview mirror. There was more traffic on the roads now, so it wasn't easy to make sure there was no one behind them.

"I hate to ask, but can we stop for something to eat before heading back?" Stacy asked.

"Of course." He glanced at her in alarm. "Are you not feeling well?"

"A little nauseous, but that happens sometimes when I'm hungry." She grimaced as she smoothed her hands over her belly. "And being at the Mexican restaurant has me longing for a large chicken quesadilla."

That made him laugh. "Far be it for me to stand between you and a quesadilla." He watched the signs as they drove, then caught a glimpse of another Mexican restaurant. "We'll stop at Horacio's Hacienda."

"Sounds great."

Marsh pulled into the parking lot a few minutes later. He quickly strode around the car to help Stacy out. "Should I grab the laptop?" she asked.

"Not here." He didn't want to attract attention. "We'll wait until we get back."

"Understood." Stacy preceded him into the restaurant.

They were provided a table and complimentary taco chips and salsa.

After they'd placed their order, he leaned forward, keeping his voice low. "You mentioned Damien's boss was Frank Gingras. I need to call Nina to see if she can dig into his background for us."

Stacy frowned. "Matt said the voice didn't sound like Frank's."

"Yeah, but he may have been wrong on that, making an assumption based on the call coming from an empty office." Marsh didn't trust Matt Wade to be objective when it came to this. The guy was far from a hired thug. "Did your husband mention anyone else at the company?"

She frowned as she considered that. "I don't think so. Wait, maybe a Justin Anderson. But I can't remember what his role was there. We'll have to go back to the Tech Guard company website to double-check." She sighed. "To be honest, I didn't pay that much attention to Damien's work. I had my own career I was managing."

"I'm not blaming you," he quickly reassured her. "It was just a question. We should have asked Matt Wade how difficult it is to get into the building."

"I can answer that. The main entrance is locked. Employees use their ID badge to scan a reader to gain access." She nibbled a chip. "There aren't any security guards on duty or anything. If someone stole a badge, I'm sure they could get in and out without anyone noticing."

"I'm sure they deactivated Dan's badge when he was let go." Marsh tried to think of another way someone could get ahold of an ID badge. "Maybe someone dropped theirs by accident. Rather than admitting their error, they simply obtained a replacement."

"That's certainly possible," Stacy agreed. "But if someone working there is involved, it would be easy enough to slip into one of the vacant offices to make the call to Matt."

"Yeah, I know." Marsh swallowed a wave of frustration. They had too many possible suspects with no way of narrowing the field.

Jackson called as their server returned with their food. He thanked her before answering. "Hey, Jackson, did Wade give you anything else to go on?"

"Afraid not." Jackson sounded frustrated, too. "I have him sitting in a hotel outside of San Antonio with strict instructions not to use his phone or any other electronic devices. As I left, he was complaining that all there was for him to do was to watch movies."

It wasn't that surprising that Matt would be annoyed by being forced to stay off grid. "We stopped for dinner," he told Jackson. "Stacy was hungry. Did you eat at La Fuentes?"

"No. And I really wanted to," Jackson said.

"Grab something to eat before you head back. We'll be on the road soon, ourselves."

"Okay. I'll call to let you know when I'm on the way back to the rental," Jackson agreed.

"Sounds good." Marsh ended the call and reached for Stacy's hand. "I think it's my turn to say grace."

Her blue eyes widened in surprise, but she simply nodded. He hadn't done this before but had heard Sam, Tucker, Leanne and Stacy pray enough to get a feeling for how it was done. "Dear Lord Jesus, we thank You for this food we are about to eat. We also thank You for keeping us safe in Your care. Please continue to watch over Stacy and her baby. Amen."

"And Marshall and Jackson, too. Amen," Stacy said.

He smiled and forced himself to release her hand. "I'm more worried about you."

"Same," she shot back, then took a bite of her quesadilla. A smile curved her lips. "It's good."

"Glad to hear it." He hoped the nourishment would make her feel better. They ate in silence for a few minutes. His mind went through the events at La Fuentes, including the moment he'd smacked Matt in the face with the laptop, causing him to drop the gun.

He should have anticipated the guy might be armed.

At the time, they were playing it cool, acting as if there wasn't a reason to be alarmed.

But he could not make a rookie mistake like that again.

"I think we need to go back to scanning my computer programs," Stacy said in a low voice. "Everyone is focused on the computer and the code. It must be in there somewhere."

"You can't think of anyplace Dan may have hidden a laptop?"

"No." She took another bite of her quesadilla. "Alex Kowalski was waiting for me when I got home. It was clear he'd searched the house and the garage."

"Okay. When we get back to the rental property we'll focus on the laptop programs." Marsh had to admit he couldn't come up with a better plan.

All he could do was hope and pray the police picked Alex Kowalski up very soon.

Thirty minutes later, they finished their meals. Marsh paid in cash as Stacy ducked into the restroom. As he escorted her outside, he glanced around, half wishing he'd asked Jackson to meet them there.

But he didn't see anything alarming as he opened Stacy's door for her. Once she was situated, he slid behind the wheel. As he pulled out of the parking lot, he made another loop around the block before heading southwest.

After driving for less than five minutes, he caught a glimpse of a dark car that could have been following them. He glanced at Stacy, unwilling to alarm her, and changed lanes.

Less than ten seconds later, the dark car behind them changed lanes, too.

He tightened his grip and hit the gas. The rental SUV

surged forward, and at the last minute, he yanked the steering wheel to get off the interstate.

"What's going on?" Stacy asked.

"There's someone behind us." He didn't dare take his eyes off the road or his rearview mirror. He quickly pulled his phone from his pocket and handed it to her. "Call Jackson. Tell him we need help."

The black car once again appeared in his rearview mirror. There was no mistaking the driver's intent as the vehicle behind them closed the gap.

"Jackson! We need help!" Stacy's voice was panicked as she provided their location. "Hurry."

Marsh was forced to stomp on the brake to avoid a car that abruptly slowed in front of him. He quickly went around it, then ran a yellow light. The dark car behind them plowed through the red light to keep pace, ignoring the blaring horns of protest.

"Who is this guy?" he muttered to himself, as he continued to drive around slower vehicles. Annoyed with the drivers, he sped through another light, then charged toward the interstate onramp.

At least on the highway he could drive faster without endangering Stacy's safety more than he already was.

After a long moment, he thought he'd lost the dark vehicle. But then, like a persistent mosquito, it appeared behind them.

Only this time, the driver went into the right-hand lane. He grimly realized the intent was to come up along Stacy's side of the car.

"Get down!" He slammed his foot on the accelerator as the driver of the dark car lowered his window, revealing a gun.

Marsh shifted his foot from the accelerator to the brake, hoping, praying the vehicle with the gunman would surge past them.

And it did, with a little help. The dark SUV was rammed from behind by another car. Marsh risked a quick glance to confirm Jackson had gotten there in time.

The dark SUV swerved, then quickly got off the interstate at the next exit. Jackson followed so Marsh didn't have to.

"It's okay, you can sit up now," he told Stacy. "Jackson has him off the freeway."

She sat upright, her complexion pale. "How did he find us?"

It was a good question. It seemed impossible.

Unless they were tracked by an electronic device?

A wave of horror washed over him. Marsh took the next exit and pulled over into the first business parking lot he could find. Then he slid out from behind the wheel and crawled beneath the SUV to examine the undercarriage.

It wasn't easy to see as the sun crept behind the horizon. He ran his fingers along the edge of the doors, then around to the rear bumper.

And that's when he found it. A small GPS tracker that had been placed on the SUV.

He pulled it free and stared at it in shock. The device had to have been planted while they were inside La Fuentes with Matt Wade.

And it was only by God's grace that Stacy hadn't been hurt or killed.

# TWELVE

That was too close. Stacy put a hand over her racing heart, knowing stress wasn't good for the baby but remaining helpless to calm her reaction. That wild ride was nearly as awful as when Marsh drove across the farmer's field to escape the gunman.

And now they'd been found again.

Marsh opened the driver's side door and got in. His brown eyes reflected his concern. "You're not hurt?"

"I'm fine." She tried to smile, but it felt more like a grimace. "I just wish I understood what was going on."

"Matt Wade's mystery caller was at La Fuentes. He put a tracking device on our car." Marsh started the engine, put the vehicle in gear and pulled out of the parking lot. "I threw it in the trash. The perp will know we found it, but I'd rather that than risk putting someone else in danger by attaching it to another vehicle."

She nodded slowly, realizing what he meant. If Marsh had placed the tracking device on a different car, the gunman could shoot first without realizing he had the wrong person. "That was the right decision."

"Yeah. Plus, I'm hoping Jackson was able to get him." Marsh headed back toward the interstate.

She took several deep breaths, willing her body to relax. "What's the plan? Are we heading back toward Lake Travis?"

Marsh took a moment to consider that before nodding. "Yeah. We're far enough away that I don't think the property location has been compromised."

"Okay." She was relieved they didn't have to find yet another place to stay.

"Where's my phone?" Marsh asked. "I'll need to call Jackson soon."

"Hang on." She bent to the side, sweeping her hand over the floorboard to search for the disposable phone. The device was wedged up against the computer that was still beneath her seat. "Got it." She sat up, then blinked when hit by a wave of dizziness.

"What's wrong?" Marsh's sharp gaze didn't miss a thing. "You swayed for a moment."

"I'm fine." She dropped the phone in the center console between them. "I just sat up too fast."

"Do you need to see your doctor?" Marsh's voice was tight with fear. "Has all this been too much for the baby?"

"I'm fine," she repeated more firmly. "It was just a brief moment of dizziness."

"I don't like it," Marsh muttered. "I don't think being dizzy is normal."

She wasn't sure whether it was, either, but she didn't think it necessary to rush to the closest hospital. At least not yet. "I have a regularly scheduled doctor's appointment next week. If the dizziness persists, I can talk to her about it then."

"Can't you call her? Talk to her about your symptoms?" Marsh did not look reassured.

"It's going on seven at night, so no. I'm not going to reach out at this hour." She sighed. "I'll be fine once I rest for a bit."

"Yeah, okay." He grudgingly dropped the issue. "Start resting now. We still have an hour of driving ahead of us until we reach Lake Travis."

Resting after that mad dash on and off the interstate seemed impossible, but she nodded and dropped her head back against the seat. Concentrating on breathing, she reminded herself there was no reason to be concerned. Marsh and Jackson had kept her safe. Marsh had found and ditched the tracking device.

And the rental property was secure.

She closed her eyes and thanked God for keeping them safe. Despite her best efforts, she couldn't fall asleep the way she had on the ride to the restaurant.

Her heart was still beating fast, likely from the aftermath of adrenaline. The baby kicked and turned, making her smile.

Thankfully her daughter was fine.

When the phone rang, she quickly reached for it, but then glanced questioningly at Marsh. He nodded. "Go ahead and answer. Just let me know what Jackson says."

"Hello? Jackson?"

"Hi, Stacy. Are you and Marsh okay?" She was touched that Jackson's first concern was for them

"We're fine. Marsh found a tracking device on the car, though. He tossed it, but now that I think about it, you may need to check your rental car, too."

"Tracking device? Planted while we were at La Fuentes?" Jackson sounded surprised. "I guess that explains how Alex Kowalski found you."

"Alex Kowalski?" She repeated for Marsh's benefit. "Are you sure? Did you arrest him?"

"Yeah, I finally caught up with him. Tell Marsh Kowalski is being held in Austin. He's refusing to talk until he gets his lawyer."

She eyed Marsh. "I'm glad Alex is in custody, even if he is refusing to talk without having a lawyer present. How long do you think that will take?"

"Not sure," Jackson said. "I'll stick around for a while to see if he changes his mind about cooperating. And I'll sweep my vehicle for a GPS device, too. But if it looks like nothing will happen until morning, I'll head back to meet up with you. Does Marsh need anything else?"

When she relayed that message, Marsh shook his head. "No, we're fine. But anything Alex Kowalski is willing to tell us would be helpful. I feel better knowing he's off the street, but I doubt he's the only guy involved."

Stacy tended to agree. She explained that to Jackson, then added, "Be careful."

"You too. Tell Marsh I'll call before heading back so he doesn't overreact when I drive in." She smiled at the note of humor in Jackson's tone.

"See you later." After disconnecting from the call, she dropped the phone back into the cupholder. Then she sighed and glanced at Marsh. "I was really hoping that arresting Alex Kowalski would be the end of this."

"He'll talk," Marsh said encouragingly. "It may take spending the night in jail, but he'll talk. He won't want to go down for attempted murder if there are others involved."

"I hope you're right." She wondered if Matt's boss, Frank Gingras, was the one who'd hired Kowalski. She frowned as a new realization popped into her mind. "I've been blaming Damien this whole time, but what if Frank is the real bad guy? Maybe Damien realized his boss was doing something illegal and stole the code to prevent him from using it?"

"That's possible," Marsh said. "Although it seems strange to me that Frank would fire Damien under that circumstance."

"Maybe he did that before he realized Dan stole the code." She wasn't sure why she was suddenly hoping Damien hadn't been the bad guy who'd put her in danger.

Marsh didn't say anything for several minutes. When he spoke, his voice was soft. "I know it's hard to imagine your husband being a criminal, but keep in mind, he could have gone to the police, the FBI or even to the higher-ups at the company if he really thought Frank was doing something illegal. Stealing the code wasn't the right answer to his dilemma."

"You're right." She turned to stare blindly out the passenger side window. Ridiculous to care what Damien did or didn't do when he was still alive. He'd lied to her about his real identity and his job. And he was gone.

A sign for Lake Travis popped into view. She noticed Marsh took the long way in getting to their street, even going so far as to pass the property, pull into another driveway and wait for several minutes before turning around to go back.

When she shot him a confused glance, he shrugged. "My way of making sure no one followed us." He stopped, then backed into the driveway.

She waited as he jumped out to open the garage, then

backed the vehicle inside. Only after he'd closed the garage door did they get out.

"I'll grab the computers," he said.

She nodded and went inside. The interior of the rental did not feel like home, but the fact that everything looked exactly as it had when they'd left made her feel safe.

Marsh came in behind her. She darted out of his way, turning toward the kitchen to make herbal tea. She must have turned too fast, because she was hit by another wave of dizziness.

When she grabbed the counter to steady herself, Marsh dropped the computers and rushed over. "Again? You were dizzy again?"

Unable to lie, she nodded.

He wrapped his arms around her and held her close. "Please call the doctor."

She rested her forehead against his chest, soaking in his warmth. As quickly as the dizziness hit, it faded away. But she was in no hurry to move from the shelter of his arms. "I'm fine. I need to stop spinning around so quickly."

"What if this is a sign of something more serious?" Marsh sounded truly upset. "I don't think we should ignore it."

"Okay, I'll call." She forced herself to lift her head and to lean back enough that she could see him. "But you know I'm probably going to end up talking to someone who doesn't even know me. That's how these things work. The OB doctors take turn being on call. I have never met my doctor's partners."

He searched her gaze. "You really want to wait until morning?"

"Yes." She reached up to touch his cheek. She wanted to reassure him she was fine, but gazing up into his dark eyes distracted her. Suddenly, she found herself lifting up on her tiptoes to kiss him.

Caught off guard by Stacy's kiss, Marsh froze for a nanosecond before pulling her closer into his arms. He'd wanted to hold her like this again since he'd rushed to her side after she was held at knifepoint. And deep down, he silently admitted he didn't want to let her go.

Their kiss was both sweetly long and far too short. When she broke away, he found it difficult to think. To figure out what to say.

"I'm sorry. I don't know what I was thinking." She looked adorably flustered.

"Please don't apologize." His voice sounded unusually husky. "I enjoyed every second."

She flushed and stepped back. "You're sweet, Marsh. I, uh, need to make some herbal tea."

He couldn't figure out if she was upset over their incredible kiss or happy about it, or embarrassed that it had happened at all. It had been so long since he'd been in a relationship that he felt rusty in reading the signs.

Besides, Stacy was pregnant, which meant—what? That she didn't know what she wanted? And really, how was he supposed to know?

He gave himself a mental shake, watching as she set about making tea. When she had finished heating her cup in the microwave, she carried it to the table and sat down. She didn't look at him as she said, "I'll pick up where I left off in going through the computer again."

"Okay. I, uh, should call Jackson." He patted his pockets, then remembered the phone was still in the car. He went back out to the garage, standing and staring up at the ceiling for a long moment before opening the driver's side door and retrieving the device.

He needed to get a grip. Stacy was going through a lot right now. Maybe he didn't understand why she'd kissed him, but he was determined not to make her feel uncomfortable.

He would be there for her, no matter what. Jackson too. And anyone else that was available to offer support.

The internal pep talk helped bring him back down to earth. Rather than reliving their kiss, Marsh needed to keep pushing the investigation forward.

In any way possible.

He headed back inside to find Stacy sitting at the table cradling her tea between her hands as she hunched over the computer. Ignoring the tripping beat of his heart, he focused on his phone.

He tried Jackson first, but his fellow ranger didn't answer. Maybe he was meeting with Kowalski and his lawyer. He next tried Nina's line. Their tech expert didn't normally work this late, so he wasn't surprised when she didn't answer, either.

But he left her a message, hoping she'd call first thing in the morning. "Nina, it's Marshall Branson. I'm calling to see if you can dig into the background of a Frank Gingras who works at Tech Guard. I don't have a date of birth, but you can estimate his age by checking out the Tech Guard website, as he's the director of operations for the company. Thanks."

With a sigh, he ended the call, found the phone charger, plugged the device in and left it on the table. From there, he went through his usual surveillance routine, moving from one window to the next to eyeball the property. The trees provided a fair amount of cover, which as he'd noted before was good and bad.

A long silence stretched between them. When he was reassured there was nothing alarming outside, he returned to the kitchen table and dropped into the chair beside Stacy. "Feeling better?"

"Hmm?" She tore her gaze from the computer. "Oh, you mean the dizziness? Yes, I'm fine. I really think it's just all the excitement that we've been through."

She could be right about that. He still wished she'd call her doctor's office but understood her concern about talking to someone she'd never met.

And to be fair, she looked better.

"The tea is helping," she said as if feeling his gaze. She glanced at him, then gestured toward the mug beside her. "I think I'm probably dehydrated. Too much crying and not enough water."

"Okay." He'd let it go for now since she was probably right about the crying part. He'd hated watching her cry. And her being dehydrated made sense. "I think you should try to get some sleep, soon, though. I can look over your computer programs. I may not be a tech expert, but I should be able to notice some abnormal code."

"You think so?" She hiked a brow. "Truthfully, I'm not even sure what we're looking for. I'm just hoping I recognize it when I see it." She shook her head wryly, then glanced at the clock. "Give me an hour, then you can take over."

"Sure thing." He pulled the second computer toward him and logged in. He was glad Jackson had asked Nina to block their IP address so they couldn't be tracked on this device, either.

He did a quick search on Frank Gingras but was disappointed to discover everything online was related to his job at Tech Guard. Running a criminal background didn't reveal anything helpful, either. The guy didn't have a record. He wasn't married or divorced and didn't have any financial judgments against him.

Nothing to indicate why Frank would have turned to a life of crime. Giving up on Frank, he turned his attention to Dan Copeland. That search also proved fruitless. No surprise really, since anything he'd found under that name would likely be fake.

He tried Damien Colter next and found even less. Sitting back in his chair, it occurred to him that US Marshal Noel Harrington must have made sure to bury the information on Damien and Geoff Colter.

Which left him with nothing more to go on.

His phone rang. Praying the call was good news from Jackson, he grabbed the device. "This is Marsh."

"Hey, it's me." Jackson sounded weary. "After meeting with his lawyer, Alex Kowalski has agreed to talk. But he wants full immunity."

"No way." Marsh glanced at Stacy, who'd looked up from her laptop. "He held a pregnant woman at knifepoint. He doesn't get a full walk on that."

"I'm glad you agree with me," Jackson said. "I told him the same thing. He'll plead to aggravated assault with a minimum sentence and tell us everything he knows about who hired him."

Marsh didn't like giving Kowalski minimum jail time,

but the deal was reasonable. "Okay, I can go along with that."

"Good. Owens said it was up to you on how much wiggle room to give Kowalski. I've already gotten approval from the DA's office, too. Now that we're all in agreement, I'll head in to talk to them now."

"Great. Please call as soon as you have information to share."

"Yeah. Keep the phone close." Jackson ended the call.

Marsh hated sitting miles away as Jackson did the negotiating and the interview with Kowalski, but it couldn't be helped. He'd pick sticking close to Stacy over leaving her with someone else anytime.

"Minimum jail time?" she asked.

"Yeah." He reached over to take her hand. "I guess we should have asked your opinion before moving forward."

"No need." She shook her head. "It's fine with me. My main concern is for the danger to be over."

"I wholeheartedly agree." He reluctantly released her hand. "After we hear from Jackson, you should try to get some sleep."

As if on cue, she yawned. "Maybe." She grimaced at the computer. "I'm starting to think I was wrong about Damien hiding the code on my laptop. I haven't found anything remotely unusual."

That wasn't good. Even with Kowalski giving them what information he knew, Marsh did not believe the danger would end until they understood what the code was all about.

And why anyone would go as far as to kill innocent people to get it back.

Stacy drained her tea, pushed away from the computer and rose to her feet. "I think you're right. I need to take a break."

He longed to pull her back into his arms but held back. She tossed her tea bag in the garbage and rinsed her cup. Then she turned to face him. "Will you wake me up if Jackson calls?"

"Of course." He stood. "Why don't you take the master bedroom? That way you'll have your own bathroom."

"Thanks. That's nice of you." She held his gaze for a long moment. "Good night." As she turned away, the phone rang.

She whirled back around, and this time, it didn't seem she was assailed by dizziness, which he took as a good sign. He picked up the phone. "Jackson?"

"Yeah, it's me. We may have made a bad deal with Kowalski."

His gut clenched. "What do you mean? He didn't know the name of the guy who hired him?"

"Yeah, but the name he gave was Noel Harrington."

"The US Marshal?" His voice rose incredulously.

"Don't worry, that proved to be wrong. We showed him a picture of the real Noel Harrington, and Kowalski claimed that wasn't the guy. He described a man in his late fifties or early sixties who was bald and had a red birthmark on the back of his neck."

"A red birthmark on the back of his neck?" Marsh repeated for Stacy's sake. Her eyes widened and the color leeched from her cheeks. Concerned, he strode toward her and took hold of her arm. "Stacy, are you okay?"

"Dan had a red birthmark on the back of his neck." Her voice wavered a bit. "He mentioned that his dad had one just like it."

Marsh understood the man who'd hired Alex Kowalski to get the code back was Geoff Colter.

Which led to the bigger question: Had Geoff murdered his own son?

# THIRTEEN

Damien's father was alive! And worse, he was a part of this nightmare. Stacy drew in a long shaky breath, doing her best to remain calm. Finding and arresting Alex Kowalski had helped provide additional information.

But the news of Geoff Colter hiring him to get the code was confusing. Were other employees at Tech Guard also involved? Or had Geoff Colter been the one to make the call to Matt Wade to get the computer?

And how had Damien and Geoff found each other after all these years? She turned toward Marsh, who'd ended his call with Jackson. "I can't believe Alex was hired by Geoff Colter. I wish I understood how Damien and his father reconnected. Was it recently? Was being reunited with his father the reason Damien stole the code?"

"I'm sure those questions will be answered once we have Colter in custody."

"You mean if we get him into custody." She ran her fingers through her hair. "The guy has eluded the US Marshals Service for years. Aren't they supposed to be good at apprehending fugitives?"

"Yeah, they are. But try not to worry." Marsh sat beside

her. "Now that we know Colter is a part of this, we may be able to set a trap for him, drawing him out of hiding."

"Really?" She held his gaze. "You think we can do that, even though we don't have the code?"

"I do, yes. Having the code would help, but we can pretend to have it."

She frowned. "He may not believe us if we can't explain how and where we found it."

"We'll make something up. Use your email or something." Marsh waved away her concern. "It's too late to come up with a plan or implement it tonight, so we'll figure something out in the morning." He reached over to take both of her hands in his. "Please, Stacy. I want you to get some sleep. It's important that you stay healthy. No more dizziness, okay?"

"I want that, too." She couldn't deny the brief episodes of unsteadiness were unusual. Logically, dehydration must be the reason. But maybe she should do a search on the symptom to see what else could be causing it. She didn't want to ignore something that could be serious. "Is Jackson heading back? Or is he staying in Austin?"

"He's on his way with the trail cameras. We'll get those put up before we take turns getting some sleep." Marsh surprised her by lifting her hands and kissing them. His warm lips sent shivers of awareness through her. A keen awareness she'd never experienced with Damien. Then Marsh released her. "Go lie down for a while. We've got things under control."

"Okay." She felt safe with Marsh and Jackson watching over her. And really, there was no way that Geoff Colter could find them at the rental property. The guy may be a tech genius, but Nina had rerouted their IP address to prevent anyone from finding them.

Marsh's idea of setting up a sting operation was intriguing. She wanted to be a part of that discussion, too. When a wide yawn caught her off guard, she realized Marsh was right about her need to sleep. For her sake, as well as the baby's.

"Good night, Marsh." She rose to her feet, secretly relieved there was no accompanying sense of dizziness. After taking a few steps toward the bedrooms, she paused to glance back at him. "You'll wake me with news?"

He hesitated, then nodded. "I'll wake you if we learn something important."

His idea of what was important may differ from hers, but she decided to let it go. With a nod, she turned and headed into the master suite.

It was nice to have the bedroom and accompanying bath to herself. Glancing out the window, she could see dozens of stars twinkling in the sky. She bowed her head and prayed that Jesus would continue to provide safety and protection for her, Marshall and Jackson. After a pause, she added another prayer for Tucker, Leanne and Pops, too.

Then she crawled into bed and promptly fell asleep.

When she awoke, the hour was early, four in the morning. The baby liked to kick her bladder, so she stood up, then nearly fell as she was hit by another wave of dizziness. She managed to grab the dresser for support and stood for a moment waiting for the dizziness to pass.

*Well, that's not good*, she thought, as she made her way to the bathroom. A few minutes later, she tiptoed out of the room to look for the computer.

Jackson was stretched out on the sofa, snoring softly. She didn't see Marsh, but the door to the second bedroom was closed, so she assumed he was sleeping in there. Without waking Jackson, she lifted the computer and carried it back to her bedroom.

Then she began to search why pregnant women may get dizzy.

According to several searches on various medical sites, she discovered that pregnant women could become dizzy especially when switching positions, like from lying to sitting up or sitting to standing. This was often a result of dehydration but could also be from anemia. The baby used a significant portion of the mother's blood supply, so it sometimes took a few minutes for her system to equilibrate.

Reassured, she set the computer aside. She didn't have her prenatal vitamins but doubted that missing one day had caused anemia. Her symptoms were likely from dehydration. She rose and went into the bathroom to drink a full glass of water. Then she returned to the bedroom. The news was reassuring. There was no need to contact her doctor. She could wait until her regularly scheduled appointment the following week.

That is, if this was over by then. She curled onto her side, trying not to think about what would happen if she had to continue burning her vacation time from work. As it was, she barely had enough time saved up to cover her maternity leave.

Thankfully, she had a small savings account that she could use if necessary. She had hoped to keep that as a backup in case she needed other days off, but she also knew Tucker and Leanne would offer some support. She would prefer to stand on her own two feet, but as a single mother, she wouldn't let pride stand in the way of meeting her daughter's needs. She would take any and all help.

She must have dozed, because the next thing she knew, daylight streamed in through the window. After washing up in the bathroom, she made her way to the kitchen.

Marsh and Jackson were drinking coffee at the table, huddled over the laptop. Marsh glanced at her, then jumped to his feet. "You look great."

"Thanks." Her cheeks heated, but she tried to ignore it. She'd slept in her clothes, which were horribly wrinkled. And she would have loved a shower. Marsh was just being nice. "What are you guys doing?"

"Examining the trail cam pics." Jackson didn't look away from the screen. "We've seen some wildlife moving around, but no sign of human intruders."

"The cameras have motion sensors," Marsh explained. "They don't turn on unless something triggers them. We've seen deer, a fox, countless rabbits and squirrels, even an owl."

"Wow." She was impressed. But then she frowned. "You're getting a lot of false alarms."

"It's not too bad." Marsh turned to glare at Jackson. "Unless you fall asleep when you're supposed to be on guard duty."

"I set the motion camera to alert my phone," Jackson said. "I woke up when the owl swooped across the screen."

She moved toward the fridge. "Would you like breakfast? We have eggs and toast."

"I'll make it." Marsh caught her hand and drew her toward the chair. "You sit. How is the dizziness this morning?"

"I'm fine." She waved a hand. "You can stop worrying. I looked it up. Dizziness is common in pregnancy and can be related to dehydration or anemia."

Marsh nodded and reached for the handle of the coffeepot to fill his cup and Jackson's. "Okay, I'll trust you to tell me if your condition worsens. Would you like tea?"

"Yes, please." She glanced at Jackson's computer screen. "That looks like the driveway."

"It is. We have four cameras total." Jackson clicked through to show her the view from each device. "We have the property well covered."

"Does this mean you're thinking of using this rental property as the home base to lure Geoff Colter?" She looked from Jackson to Marsh.

Jackson's phone rang. "Hold that thought." He hesitated and glanced at Marsh. "It's Noel Harrington, I gave him the number of my disposable phone. You want me to take it here? Or drive away from here and call him back?"

"You can stay here and answer it." Marsh shrugged. "We know Geoff Colter is involved, and Harrington knows him better than anyone else. We need his input on the guy."

"Got it." Jackson lifted the phone. "Hey, Noel. What's going on?"

Stacy couldn't hear the other side of the conversation. Marsh brought her tea. She smiled in thanks, cradling the mug between her hands.

"Yeah, that's correct," Jackson said. "Alex Kowalski described the guy who hired him as having a red birthmark on the back of his neck. According to Stacy, Damien had one just like it." Jackson paused, then added, "Interestingly, Geoff Colter is using your name. Or at least he did with Alex Kowalski."

"What?" Noel's shout was loud enough to be heard across the room. Wincing, Jackson held the phone from his ear. "Me? That lowlife implicated me?"

"We know he's lying," Jackson said placatingly. "And we have an idea of how to approach this. But I don't want to get into that now. Marsh and I need to talk things through with our boss first. We'll be in touch later, okay?"

Noel Harrington must have agreed, because Jackson ended the call and tossed the phone onto the table. "Wow. I may have lost some hearing in my ear."

"He has a right to be mad." Stacy sipped her tea, then set it aside. "Colter has some nerve using the name of a US Marshal to hire a thug to attack a pregnant woman."

"True. That's absolutely a slap in the face." Marsh pulled eggs from the fridge and set them beside a large frying pan. "How do you like them?"

As Marsh cooked breakfast, she retrieved her laptop from the bedroom and tried to think of another place to look for the mystery code.

"Hey, maybe we should see if your tech expert, Nina, can find it?" Stacy set the computer aside as Marsh carried their plates to the table. "Because I've tapped out my areas of expertise."

"That's not a bad thought," Marsh agreed. "We'll discuss that later. For now, I'd like to say grace."

She nodded and bowed her head. Beneath the edge of the table, Marsh took her hand in his.

"Dear Lord Jesus, please bless this food we are about

to eat. We humbly ask that You continue to keep all of us safe in Your care. Amen."

"Amen," she and Jackson echoed. She released Marsh's hand and began to eat, knowing she needed strength to face the day ahead.

Somehow, she sensed this nightmare would be over sooner rather than later. And she silently added another prayer that they would all escape unscathed from whatever plan they'd come up with to draw Geoff Colter in and then to arrest him.

Marsh and Jackson had argued earlier that day about the best way to approach the plan to draw Colter out of hiding. Marsh wanted to get a female police officer to the property to pretend to be Stacy.

Jackson was afraid that Colter would recognize the woman as a ploy and would avoid taking the bait.

They did agree that they could not in good conscience ask a pregnant police officer to impersonate Stacy. The female cop would have to pretend to be pregnant. And possibly dye her hair to match Stacy's dark tresses.

The two men had also agreed not to discuss the plan with Stacy until they'd run several scenarios past their captain, John Owens.

When they finished eating, Jackson offered to do the dishes. Marsh gestured to Stacy's computer. "You really think Nina can find the code?"

"I don't know." Stacy sighed. "I feel like I'm missing something obvious, but I've looked everywhere I can think of that Dan may have used as a hiding spot."

"Nina is amazing," Jackson said from his position at the kitchen sink. "I'm sure she can find it."

"I'm not sure I want either of us to drive back to Austin just yet." Reviewing the camera photos had convinced Marsh they were safe there for the first time in what seemed like forever. He wasn't eager to change that even though Stacy's comment about using this place as the location to lure Colter out of hiding was a good idea.

With the trail cameras, they'd see the guy coming well before he could get close to the house.

"Oh, wow. Baby is active today." Stacy placed her palms over her abdomen. "Usually she waits until I want to fall asleep."

He leaned forward, wishing he could share the wonder of the moment with her. "Are you still thinking about naming your daughter Eleanor?"

"I haven't given it any more thought since we spoke about it." She shrugged. "I like my mother's name, but it's rather old-fashioned. That's what's holding me back from making Eleanor her first name."

"Keep in mind, old-fashioned names are making a comeback," Marsh pointed out. "All that matters is whether you like it. Not what anyone else thinks."

"You're right." She eyed him curiously. "What's your mother's name?"

"Catherine." He grinned. "Another old-fashioned name."

She nodded, her expression thoughtful. "I probably need to give it more thought. Although I've also wondered if I should wait until the baby is born. Maybe a name will pop into my mind the minute I see her."

He smiled. "I'm sure a name will come to you. And there is plenty of time. To be honest, I really like Eleanor."

"Ellie," she whispered. "The name is growing on me."

Marsh longed to draw her up and into his arms for a

kiss. Instead, he stood and moved to look out the window and at the wooded scenery beyond. He had been betrayed by a woman, much the way Stacy had been lied to by her husband. He hadn't intended to fall in love again.

But somehow, he was dangerously close to doing just that.

Maybe once Tucker punched his lights out, his buddy would get over the fact that Marsh wanted to date his little sister.

His pregnant little sister.

He winced. What was he thinking?

"Marsh, do you think this will be over by next week Tuesday?" Stacy asked.

He turned from the window to face her. "Is that your next doctor's appointment?"

"Yes." She turned toward the computer and opened a photo. Marsh crossed over to see it.

"Oh, is that your sonogram?" He had personally never seen one up close.

"Yes. See, here's her head." Stacy drew on the image with her fingertip. "And her tiny body is here. Hard to see, but you can follow the line of her spine."

"Wow. I can't get over how tiny she is." He wasn't about to mention the baby looked way smaller on the picture compared to the size of her belly. Then he realized this picture was taken a while ago. "How far along were you when this was done?"

"Fourteen—" She abruptly stopped. "Wait a minute. I think I found it!"

"What? The code?" He frowned. "Where?"

"Here. Right here, where I should have looked in the beginning." Her tone was laced with bitterness. "I can't believe it. That jerk actually used this picture of our baby to hide his stolen code!"

"Where?" He still wasn't following. "Show me."

"It's within the image itself." She turned the computer, then used the keyboard to enlarge the picture. Then she pointed the cursor toward the top of the photo.

And that's when he saw it. A series of digits all in a row that had been used to rename the sonogram. He turned to meet her gaze. "You didn't notice until now?"

"No, because I've had this up on my desktop since I first opened it." She sounded upset with herself. "I haven't had to do a search to pull it up. If I had done that, I'd have noticed the new name right away. Or rather would have noticed that the image of 'Copeland-Stacy-Baby' didn't exist anymore because it had been changed to this random series of numbers."

He nodded in understanding, although there was nothing random about the digits on the screen. "How many numbers is that?"

"A lot." Stacy shook her head and quickly counted. "Twenty-seven. Too many for most bank accounts, or even a key code."

Jackson came over, drying his hands on a dish towel. "Twenty-seven digits also seems too short for a software code. Those can go on for pages, can't they?"

"In my experience, yes. But if this is related to something Damien and his father did ten years ago?" Stacy shook her head. "I have no idea what was used back then."

"But we're operating under the assumption the code was stolen recently." Marsh stared at the series of numbers. "Maybe they're for a foreign bank account? People try to hide money by using Swiss bank accounts or even accounts down in the Cayman Islands."

"That could be." Stacy highlighted and copied the code, then pasted it into a search engine. She hit the Enter key, but nothing came up.

"Try searching on what a series of twenty-seven numbers might mean," he suggested. "Maybe that will help narrow down the possibilities."

"Okay." She typed in the request. The first few responses were vague. Then, as she scrolled down the screen, it popped out at him.

Cryptocurrency is identified by a series of numbers from 25 to 36 digits long.

"Cryptocurrency?" he repeated, stunned by the revelation. "You really think so?"

Stacy frowned, slowly nodding. "That seems the most logical, considering the lengths that have been taken to access the information. I'm sure this code must be a link to sending or receiving cryptocurrency funds." She sat back in her chair. "And Damien must have stolen it from his father or from someone at Tech Guard. I still can't figure out which one."

Marsh exchanged a long look with Jackson. His Texas Ranger buddy shook his head and lifted his hands in a palms-up gesture. Marsh silently agreed with his sentiment. Cryptocurrency and sales on the dark web were well outside their wheelhouse. Rangers didn't usually handle stuff like this. They'd have to get the feds involved to understand how much money was at stake. He didn't even know what the cryptocurrency exchange rate was.

Yet he sensed there was a lot of money involved, since one man had already been murdered. Possibly others that they weren't even aware of.

Either way, he suspected Geoff Colter wasn't about to let anyone get in his way of retrieving what he believed was rightfully his.

And Marsh wanted Stacy to be far away when that confrontation took place.

# FOURTEEN

Acid roiled in her stomach as Stacy realized Damien had chosen their baby's sonogram as the place to hide his stolen code.

Something he must have known would place her and their baby in danger!

Had her husband ever loved her? He'd told her so many lies, she honestly wasn't sure. Staring at the sonogram image that had once been titled Copeland-Stacy-Baby but was now a series of numbers, she curled her fingers into fists. How could he have done such a thing?

But getting mad at a dead man was useless. Damien was gone and never coming back. She struggled to rein in her temper, desperately wishing for the first time that she'd never met or married Dan/Damien.

No, that wasn't true. She winced, doing her best to calm down. No stress, remember? She drew in a long cleansing breath, unclenched her hands and smoothed her palms over her belly. There was no way she would ever regret having her baby daughter. Even if that meant raising her little girl alone.

But being safe didn't seem like too much to ask, either.

"Okay, so we have the code," Marsh said, interrupting

her thoughts. "We need Nina or someone from the tech team to help us figure out what to do with it."

"I'll call her," Jackson offered.

Stacy turned toward Marsh. "Does it matter what the code is used for? I mean, isn't the point of this to lure Geoff Colter out of hiding? Now that we have the code, we can do that by telling him exactly where we found it." She swallowed hard. "How Damien had hidden the code in the sonogram image. I have a feeling Geoff Colter will be impressed by his ingenuity."

"Yeah, I see your point." He grimaced. "But if this code leads to stolen money, we are obligated to figure out the source."

She frowned. But then realization dawned. "There may be others out there who know about the stolen cryptocurrency, if that's what this is."

"That's one possibility. The other is related to whatever goods were sold that resulted in the payment." Marsh shook his head. "I think there are a lot of potential theories we could envision. And let's not forget that Matt Wade from Tech Guard was involved. We can't rule out that someone from the company is the originator of the cryptocurrency."

Marsh was right, the endless scenarios were making her head hurt. "Damien may have discovered that something was being sold out of Tech Guard and took it upon himself to steal the cryptocurrency code to get the money for himself. But if that were true, how did his father fit into the picture?"

"I don't know. I'm wondering the same thing. Because clearly Colter was the guy who hired Alex Kowalski to attack you." Marsh watched as Jackson walked to the other side of the living room to make his call to Nina. "That's why we need additional resources on this."

She was almost afraid to ask about the plan related to drawing Geoff Colter out of hiding. Glancing around the interior of their rental home, she had to admit she'd enjoyed her time being there. The scenery was beautiful. And she had Marsh and Jackson watching over her, along with cameras mounted outside to warn them of any potential threat.

Deep down, she didn't want to leave.

As if reading her mind, Marsh said, "We're going to set up a conference call with Noel Harrington and our boss John Owens to discuss our next steps. I don't want you to worry, there's no way we'll risk putting you in danger."

"I don't want to be in danger, either, but if it's easier to use me to draw Geoff out of hiding, then that's what we should do." She held Marsh's gaze. "Whatever it takes, Marsh. I want this to be over."

"We'll figure it out." His dark eyes hardened. "But I can guarantee we're not going to let Colter or his accomplice, if he has one, come anywhere near you."

"Okay. I'll go along with whatever you decide." She understood there was no point in arguing. Marsh would not budge, and if she were honest, she loved him for that.

Wait, not *love* love. She loved him as a friend. Her brother's friend. The man who'd put his life on the line for hers.

Not romantically.

Yet when she glanced at his rugged profile, his blond hair and dark eyes, she realized she was fooling herself. Her feelings for Jackson, who was just as kind and willing to put his life on the line for her, were nothing like those she harbored for Marsh. She cared about Jackson as a friend.

Her attraction for Marsh emanated from a visceral level.

And kissing him had only reinforced her growing feelings for him. Maybe it was her pregnancy hormones running rampant or the intensity of the situation and the danger surrounding them, but there was no doubt in her mind that she was falling hard for her brother's best friend.

"Stacy?" She startled when Jackson called her name. "Can you send that picture to Nina?"

"Of course." She reached for the computer, pulling it close. "What's her email?"

Jackson crossed over and provided her the information, watching over her shoulder as she typed it in. Then she attached the image of the sonogram to the message and sent it.

"Thanks." Jackson flashed a smile, then turned away. "Nina? You should have it any second."

"Would you like more herbal tea?" Marsh stood. "I'm happy to make it for you."

His caring gesture made tears prick her eyes. "Yes, thanks." She turned and subtly wiped the moisture away. Time to get a grip on her emotions. "I'd like to be a part of that conference call with Noel."

"Of course." Marsh busied himself in the kitchen, making her tea. Something Damien never would have done.

Giving herself a mental shake, she pushed the computer away. She needed to stop comparing the two men. That task was as pointless as getting angry with Damien for what he'd done.

His lies. Stealing the code. Putting her in harm's way.

She abruptly realized that if Damien hadn't done those things, she wouldn't have had this time alone with Marsh. Wouldn't have gotten to know him even better than when they'd been together at the Rocking T Ranch. It made her smile to remember how she'd taught him how to do the ranch chores. Poor guy had never mucked out a stall in his life prior to that.

She remembered when she'd attended church a few weeks after Damien's murder. The pastor had spoken at length about the Lord's plan for them. How they needed to trust in His judgment. In His plan. And in His word.

She needed to take that sermon to heart.

"Here you go." Marsh brought a steaming mug of herbal tea to the table.

"Thank you." She took the mug, cradling the warmth in her hands. "You've been wonderful through all of this, Marsh. I can't thank you enough."

He looked surprised, then frowned. "No need to thank me. This is our job as rangers."

Had she offended him in some way? Before she could ask, Jackson turned back to face them. "Owens wants to talk to us first prior to adding the others. He has time now. Otherwise, we have to wait until after his meeting with the governor."

"Now is fine," Marsh agreed. "Better we work out the kinks prior to his meeting, anyway."

"I'd like to listen in," Stacy said.

"Fine with me." Jackson eyed Marsh, who shrugged and nodded.

When Jackson's phone rang, he answered. "Yeah, Captain, hang on. I'm putting the call on speaker so Marsh and Stacy can participate." He punched a few keys on the basic cell phone, then set it on the kitchen table.

Marsh sat beside her. She reached for his hand, glad when his strong warm fingers wrapped around hers as Jackson filled Owens in on what they knew so far. Including the code that was likely related to cryptocurrency.

Stacy listened, comforted by the fact that they had senior leadership support on their plan.

Surely nothing could go wrong with everyone operating out of the same playbook.

"We need to move Stacy to a different location," Marsh said when Jackson had finished updating their boss. "Her safety is our top priority."

"Why not just keep her there at the rental property?" Owens asked.

"I think the rental is the best place to use for the trap," Marsh explained. "My thought is that we keep her computer at this rental house location, with the code imbedded in her sonogram picture. Nina can talk us through how to get rid of the IP address rerouting she placed on the device. Once we have eliminated that hurdle, we log into the internet via Stacy's computer. I suspect Geoff Colter is skilled enough to quickly track the device to this location, which will appear to be a great hiding spot for Stacy. That may convince him to head over to retrieve the code."

"And what if he doesn't come himself?" Owens asked. "For all we know, he could send a bunch of foot soldiers to do his bidding."

"We can run that question past Noel Harrington," Marsh said. "He knows Colter the best. But somehow, I don't think Geoff has an army working with him." He glanced at Jackson questioningly. "Kowalski didn't give out any other names of accomplices, did he?"

"Correct. Kowalski did not give up anyone else as being involved. But he also didn't admit to killing Damien Colter, either." Jackson sighed. "Either Kowalski lied about that, or Geoff killed his own son. We can try to interview Kowalski again, but in the meantime, we should err on the side of caution and assume Colter could have at least one other guy working with him. Maybe two."

Marsh thought about how often they'd been tailed and found by a gunman. It was hard to imagine Colter doing all of that alone. "I agree, we should anticipate at least one other player, maybe two. Which means this rental property is still the best option. There's plenty of woods surrounding the place, it's isolated, but with the cameras in place, we'll see anyone approaching long before they see us."

"And where would you like to keep Ms. Copeland?" Owens asked.

That was the million-dollar question in Marsh's mind. He would have liked nothing more than to participate in springing the trap on Colter and his accomplices, but he would not leave Stacy alone. No matter where she was located.

He would be right there with her. Even if that meant leaving the takedown to others.

"Maybe a rental property nearby?" Jackson suggested when Marsh didn't answer. "Or we find a motel outside of Lake Travis to use as a temporary safe house."

"Maybe I should just stay here," Stacy interjected.

"Not happening." Marsh glared at her. "Owens, we'll

need another man here inside the rental property to team up with Noel Harrington and Jackson. Is Sam available?"

"Yes, I've arranged for Sam to hand off his current case to another ranger," Owens said. "He'll be back in the Austin area by the end of the day."

"Okay, so that means we can't implement our plan until later tonight." Marsh wasn't sure it was smart to set the trap while it was dark outside. Then again, Colter was probably more likely to show up in the middle of the night regardless of when they sprung the trap.

"We need to coordinate with Noel Harrington, too," Jackson said. "He may want to bring others in to support the arrest of Geoff Colter."

"Wait, what exactly is Geoff being arrested for?" Stacy glanced at Marsh, then at Jackson. "Hasn't the statute of limitations run out on his hacking crimes from ten years ago?"

"Yes, the statute of limitations for hacking into government systems is ten years," Owens confirmed. "However, we don't know what Colter did with the information he and his son obtained. Depending on where they sold the data and what may have transpired since that interaction took place, we can hold him on potential espionage charges."

"And if we can figure out what the cryptocurrency is related to, we may find more charges to levy against him," Marsh added. "All the more reason we probably need the feds involved."

"Did we ever figure out who those federal agents were that showed up on the ranch?" Stacy asked.

Marsh grimaced. "No, but now that you mention it, I think we should get photos of both Kowalski and Geoff

Colter over to Leanne to make sure they weren't the imposters."

"We don't have an updated image of Geoff Colter," Jackson pointed out. "We can use a computer generated one, but those aren't always as accurate as we'd like, at least according to Nina. For sure we can send Kowalski's mug shot."

"Do it," Owens said. "And once we have Colter in custody, we can see if Leanne recognizes him, too." There was a brief pause before his boss asked, "Anything else?"

"We can take it from here," Marsh said. "I'll arrange for a new location for Stacy. Then we'll reach out to Harrington to update him."

"Sounds good. Keep me in the loop." Owens ended the call.

Jackson picked up his phone from the table. "I'll reach out to Harrington. You find a place for Stacy."

Marsh let Jackson make the call, which ended up going to voice mail anyway. He used Stacy's computer to search on properties in the Lake Travis region and found a second rental house that wasn't too far away. "How is this place?" He turned the screen to show her.

"I'm not picky." She barely glanced at the photos. "If that works for you, it's fine with me."

He nodded and used the rental property program to make the arrangements. He hesitated, knowing their plan was to stay off grid, but then decided that Colter would be more interested in finding Stacy's computer. He went ahead and used the Texas Ranger account to obtain the rental.

"When will you move me to the new property?"

Marsh's heart squeezed at the apprehension in Stacy's gaze. "I can be ready anytime."

"Actually, we can't get in until late afternoon." He offered a reassuring smile. "Try not to worry. We'll take precautions in getting you moved to the new house."

"I know, I'm not worried." She rose to her feet. "Like I said earlier, I just want this to be over."

When she disappeared into her bedroom, he was struck by the need to follow her to make sure she wasn't about to cry again but then reminded himself that she also deserved privacy.

The sound of a ringing phone caught him off guard. He glanced over to see Jackson holding up the device. "It's Harrington," he said before answering the call. "Hey, Noel. Thanks for calling me back."

Jackson listened for a moment, then joined Marsh. "Yeah, just a minute." He put the call on speaker again. "We're here at the rental house. We have a plan to lure Geoff Colter out of hiding. Are you interested in being part of the takedown?"

"Absolutely," Noel said without hesitation. "Where are you? I'll head over to join you."

Marsh frowned and shook his head. Oddly, he didn't want Harrington to get there until he'd moved Stacy to the new safe house.

"I'll get you the address to the property soon, but let's walk through the plan," Jackson said, then briefed the marshal on the idea of using Stacy's computer containing the stolen code to draw Colter out of hiding.

"You found the code?" Harrington sounded shocked. "That's great news. I need you to send a copy to me, ASAP."

"I will do that in a bit," Jackson said. "But for now, is there anyone else from the Marshals Service that you want included in this?"

There was a pause as Noel considered that. "Depends on how quickly you want to implement the takedown. I can have guys here by tomorrow morning if needed."

"Tomorrow is too long," Marsh said. "I would rather get the ball rolling tonight."

"Tonight works for me. We can ask local cops to lend a hand," Noel said. "Or if you'd rather not get others in the loop, I'm sure the three of us can handle one old man."

"You don't think he has accomplices?" Marsh asked.

"I don't know, maybe." Noel sounded impatient. "You told me you already have one of them in custody. He's the guy who claimed I was involved, right? But then described a much older guy who we believe is Colter. So really, how many others could there be?"

The guy's casual approach set Marsh's teeth on edge, but he knew some federal agents had an attitude that made them think they were better than anyone else.

"We want to be prepared for anything," Jackson said, sensing Marsh's annoyance. "Are you still in Austin?"

"Yep. I can meet you anytime," Noel said.

"We'll call you back," Jackson assured him. "We're waiting for another ranger pal of ours to get here."

"Sounds good," Noel said. "I'm anxious to get Colter. We need to know if he sold any of the information he hacked to our enemies."

"Okay, we'll be in touch," Jackson said. Then quickly ended the call.

"Thanks for not giving out the address." Marsh grimaced. "I'm probably being overprotective, but I want Stacy far away from here before the information gets out."

"Understood." Jackson rose to grab the computer linked to the cameras. "I think we need to focus our attention on the front and back entrances to the house." He indicated the two cameras in question. "They're the most logical place to attempt to gain access."

"Yeah, okay." Marsh glanced at his watch. It was still early, barely ten in the morning. He rose and went down the hall to listen outside the door of Stacy's room. When he didn't hear any crying, he returned to the kitchen. "This is going to be a long day."

"No lie," Jackson muttered. "Let's get the mug shot of Alex Kowalski to Leanne. Those guys who showed up at the ranch are bugging me."

"Me too." Marsh watched as Jackson accessed his work computer to obtain the mug shot and send it to Tucker. Then he made another call. "Tuck? Have Leanne check this guy out. See if he's one of those who showed up at the Rocking T."

There was a moment of silence. Then Jackson frowned. "Not the same guy? Okay, thanks." He lowered the phone, shaking his head. "Well, that's not good. Leanne is positive Alex Kowalski is not one of the two men who showed up at the ranch claiming to be a fed."

Marsh narrowed his gaze. "Maybe they really were with the Department of Defense? Maybe they know something about where the hacked information ended up?"

"But then, why not simply work with us?" Jackson asked. "Why refuse to let Leanne examine their credentials?"

That bothered Marsh, too. "I have no idea. I think the

entire thing is rather strange." He stood and crossed to the kitchen counter. "I'll make another pot of coffee. I have a feeling we're going to need a lot of caffeine to get through the day."

"Yeah." Jackson yawned widely. "Especially me."

Marsh kept an eye on Stacy's bedroom door, growing more concerned the longer she stayed inside. Granted, she may be doing nothing more than taking a well-deserved nap. Still, he couldn't squelch the need to check on her.

He walked toward the door when Jackson abruptly said, "Marsh! Someone's coming!"

He spun to face him. "Who?"

"A dark green Jeep." Jackson pulled his weapon from his holster. "You take the back. I'll cover the front."

Marsh strode quickly to rap on Stacy's door. "Stacy? You need to stay inside your room, okay?"

"What's going on?" Her voice was tinged with fear.

"Just stay inside. I'll come for you when it's safe." He glanced at Jackson, then hurried toward the back door.

A second later, it was kicked open, revealing a masked man holding a gun.

# FIFTEEN

"Drop it!" Stacy heard Marsh's sharp command moments before the crack of gunfire.

Not just one shot but several. Her heart froze in her chest, every muscle on high alert as she fought the urge to scream.

*No! Not Marsh! Please, Lord Jesus, not Marsh!*

Fearful for what was happening outside the bedroom, she realized she couldn't just stand here. She had no idea how many bad guys were out there. She needed a weapon!

Feeling desperate, she hurried into the bathroom. She'd used the bathroom as a refuge before, but this time she didn't want to just crawl into the tub. Thinking fast, she closed and locked the door behind her, then rushed over to lift the ceramic piece up off the back of the toilet tank.

It was heavy. But she didn't let that stop her. She picked it up and stepped behind the bathroom door. With trembling arms, she held the top of the tank up over her head, imagining bringing it down on the assailant's head.

Seconds ticked by with excruciating slowness. When she knew she couldn't hold that toilet tank cover up one minute longer, she heard Marsh's voice.

"Stacy? Are you okay?"

"Yes!" She lowered the heavy ceramic piece so that it hit the floor with a thud. But she still didn't move. She waited until she heard Marsh's voice coming closer.

"Stacy?" He rattled the door handle. "You can come out now."

She stepped over the tank cover and shakily unlocked the door. She opened it and nearly fell into Marsh's arms.

"You're not hurt?" she asked in a choked voice.

"It's just a graze." He wrapped his arms around her, pulling her close. "We have two men in custody. Well, technically one man in custody, as the younger guy is dead."

She shivered, pressing her face into his chest for a moment as the realization of how close Marsh and Jackson had come to being hurt hit hard. She silently thanked Jesus for keeping them safe, then gathered her strength and pushed back enough to look up at him. "I don't understand. How did they find us?"

"I don't know." Marsh's expression was grim. "But we're going to get you out of here in case these guys weren't acting alone."

"Okay."

He surprised her by pressing a quick kiss against her mouth. But he released her too quickly for her to enjoy it. "Jackson is calling Owens."

She belatedly noticed the dark red blood matting his upper arm. "We need to take care of your wound."

"Later." He didn't bother to glance at the injury. "It's just a graze," he repeated.

Knowing arguing was useless, she allowed Marsh to draw her from the master suite. Jackson stood in the hallway talking on the phone.

"Yeah, we absolutely need to understand how we were found," Jackson said, his gaze grim. "We have one down and one in custody."

Craning her neck, she could see that one man was lying on the ground in a pool of blood. Her stomach rolled and she quickly tore her gaze away, fearing she'd throw up.

"I'm taking Stacy outside to the other rental," Marsh told Jackson.

"The Jeep is blocking the driveway," Jackson said. Then added, "Yeah, boss, I could use Nina's help with figuring out who may have been able to track the computer or our disposable phones."

"Jeep?" She glanced at Marsh. "They drove up to the house?"

"One guy drove, the other must have come in on foot to approach the back." Marsh looked upset. "I'm not sure how he avoided the cameras."

"No one knew about them other than your boss, right?" She was still trying to come to grips with how on earth the bad guys had found the rental property. "Are you sure we can trust him? Your boss, I mean."

"Owens has dedicated his life to the Texas Rangers," Marsh said somberly. "I've never once had reason to doubt his integrity."

She winced. "Okay, sorry. I just don't know what to think about all of this."

"Me either." Marsh drew her into the living room. "Recognize him?"

Her eyes widened in shock. "Harold Green!" Then realization hit hard. "No, you're not a widower at all, are you? You're Damien's father, Geoff Colter."

"Widower?" Marsh looked confused for a moment.

Then his expression cleared. "The night you were attacked, you mentioned coming home from a widow support group. You even mentioned a widower named Harold Green."

"Yes, I knew him by that name. And for several weeks Harold here would talk to me. Try to make me feel better about losing my husband. Telling me so many stories about the love of his life, his wife of thirty years."

To her horror, Geoff Colter grinned. "Yeah, poor little Stacy. All tore up over Damien's death."

"You killed him!" She took a step closer, but Marsh snagged her arm, holding her back. "How could you kill your own son?"

"I didn't kill him," Colter denied flatly. "But if you ask me, Damien deserved what he got after agreeing to testify against me. What son treats his father that way?"

His words were like a slap to the face. She put her hand over her rounded belly, praying her daughter would not take after Geoff or Damien Colter.

"You're despicable," she said harshly.

"Don't waste your breath talking to him." Marsh slid his arm around her waist. "Let's get out of here."

She forced herself to turn away from Geoff Colter. She couldn't bear to think about how close they'd all come to dying today. Marsh urged her forward, pausing long enough to reach for her laptop.

The one containing her baby's sonogram picture.

She looked at Marsh. "I almost wish I had simply saved the image to another name. That I erased every last digit of the code, forever."

"We'll get to do that soon," he said, handing the laptop case to her. "I'm sorry, but you'll need to carry this so I can keep my hands free."

"That's fine." She took the case from him and looped the strap over her shoulder. It was far lighter than the ceramic top of the toilet. "I'm ready."

"Which way are you going?" Jackson asked.

"I'm debating," Marsh admitted. "I think we should go out the back. Maybe cut through the woods to the next property before we head up to the road. I feel like the longer we can stay hidden, the better."

"Good plan. I'll stay here until Owens sends reinforcements." Jackson grimaced at Geoff Colter. "I should probably call Noel Harrington, too. He'll want to interview our pal, here."

"You know where to find us." Marsh took her arm and steered her toward the back door. "But don't tell anyone else, understand?"

"Got it," Jackson called as they edged past the dead man. Stacy's stomach clenched, but she managed to swallow against the surge of nausea.

The outside air was warmer than she'd expected. Or maybe her heart was racing so fast she didn't notice the February breeze. She rested her right hand on the computer case as Marsh led her into the woods.

She was surprised to find the area was dense with foliage. There was nothing that appeared to be a path. Marsh went first, holding branches out of the way for her. She followed his lead, keeping an eye on the ground to make sure she didn't trip over tree roots or rocks.

When a hand roughly grabbed her arm, she drew in a breath to scream.

Then felt the muzzle of a gun pressing against her temple.

She froze, her breath locked in her throat. When the man who held her yanked the computer case off her shoulder, she let it go without saying a word.

But Marsh must have known, because he abruptly turned, bringing his weapon up. His dark eyes hardened. "Let her go."

"Don't miss, you might hit the pretty pregnant woman," a voice said. She didn't recognize it, but from the horrified expression in Marsh's gaze, he recognized the assailant.

"Why?" Marsh asked harshly. "You're a US Marshal sworn to uphold the law!"

US Marshal? Noel Harrington? She didn't dare move, deathly afraid Harrington would shoot her right then and there.

"Yeah, and what do I have to show for it?" Harrington's voice was harsh. "My ex-wife took half of everything I own, and I'm in debt to a loan shark for the rest. I've spent my entire life protecting worthless criminals, so yeah, I'll take the cryptocurrency code, cash in and get out of here once and for all. Now drop your gun or I'll shoot."

"You don't want to hurt a pregnant woman." Marsh's tone was reasonable, when she feared there was nothing remotely rational in the man holding her. "Let her go and you can have the code."

"I'm not stupid. I'll take the code regardless. Drop the gun. Or this ends here." Harrington pressed the tip of the gun harder against her temple, making her wince. "Now! I'm not asking again."

Marsh abruptly nodded and lifted his weapon so that it was pointing up at the sky. "Okay, you win. I'm going to throw my gun into the woods. There's no reason for you to hurt her. She's not going to stop you."

When Marsh tossed his gun aside, the pressure on her temple eased. Then with an abrupt move, Harrington shoved her forward. She stumbled over a tree root, trying to avoid hitting the ground. Marsh instinctively reached out to her.

The sound of a gunshot had her ducking down as she fell into Marsh's arms.

"He's down." Jackson's voice was strained. After a moment he added, "And unfortunately, he's dead. I'd rather he spent the rest of his miserable life in jail. Are you both okay?"

"Yes," she managed, burying her face against Marsh's chest. As he held her close, she was torn between a wave of overwhelming relief at knowing the danger was finally over and the keen despair over knowing her time with Marsh was also coming to an end.

She snaked her arms around his waist and held on tight, wishing she never had to let him go.

Marsh crushed Stacy against him, his heart thundering so loudly he could barely hear Jackson.

"I stood over Colter thinking that the only way we could have been found is if Harrington had tracked our most recent phone call," Jackson was saying. "I left him cuffed and came straight out here to find the idiot holding Stacy at gunpoint. I'm glad you noticed me and kept him distracted long enough so I could take him out."

"I did see you and was glad you'd come to find us." Marsh locked gazes with his fellow ranger. "Thank you. Your smart thinking and timing were perfect."

"I still can't believe he was dirty." Jackson scowled, shaking his head. "I mean sure, he said he had money problems, but to do something like this? That's pathetic."

"Yeah, well, most criminals are pathetic. And greedy. And maybe the years of protecting criminals made him think it would be easier to grab some cash and take off." Marsh couldn't believe how close he'd come to losing Stacy. He didn't want to let her go, but they couldn't stand out here forever. "Stacy? Are you okay to keep going?"

"Yes." Her voice was muffled against his shirt. She tightened her hold on him, then finally lifted her head. "It's over for real, right?"

"Yes, I think so." He hesitated, loath to take her back inside where Geoff Colter was. But then the wail of police sirens split the air.

"Someone called in the sound of gunfire," Stacy murmured. She lifted her head to look up at Marsh. "We need to stay and tell them what's happened."

He admired her strength so much it was all he could do not to kiss her again. But this wasn't the time to talk about the future.

Their future.

Not when they had to tie up the loose ends of this mess. The worst of the danger was over, but there were several questions that still needed to be answered.

"Okay, let's go back inside." He had to raise his voice to carry over the sirens that were incredibly loud now. He scanned the woods to his right, where he'd tossed his weapon. He found and retrieved the gun, knowing he'd have to hand it over to the cops who were about to converge on the scene. After all, he'd shot and killed the younger thug who'd entered the back door of the rental house.

He bent and snagged the computer from where it sat partially beneath Harrington's dead body. The feds would be all over this, he thought with a sigh as he urged Stacy up toward the house. He and Jackson had discharged their weapons, resulting in the death of two perps. Officer involved shootings were never good.

Worse when one of the dead men was a US federal marshal.

The cops rushed toward them weapons raised. "Stop! Hands up where we can see them!"

"We're rangers," Jackson said, lifting his hands. "Two Texas Rangers on duty. I'll show you my badge if you let me pull it from my pocket."

The cops exchanged a look, then nodded. Jackson pulled his badge first, and Marsh mirrored his movements.

"What happened?" One of the officers gaped when he caught a glimpse of Harrington's dead body. "Who shot him?"

"I did," Jackson admitted.

"But for a good reason. It's a long story." Marsh stepped forward. "We'll explain everything after we go inside where Mrs. Copeland can sit and rest."

The debriefing with the local police didn't take long, but then Owens and Sam Hayward arrived, forcing Marsh and Jackson to go through the entire scenario again.

"Damien Colter must have stolen the cryptocurrency code from someone else, and we're not sure who he double crossed." A glance at Geoff made him think Damien had taken the code from his old man, but the elder Colter remained stubbornly silent. "There are two additional pieces of the puzzle that we need," Marsh continued. "We don't know if anyone at Tech Guard is involved or the identity of the two men who went to the Rocking T claiming to be with the federal government."

"Give me a minute," Jackson said, using his regular phone now that they were surrounded by law enforcement officials. Jackson took a picture of the dead man who'd come in through the back door, then took another of Geoff Colter. "I'll send photos of the three perps we have here to Tucker and Leanne," Jackson said. "Maybe they'll recognize one of them."

"Send a picture of Harrington, too," Marsh suggested. He glanced at Stacy, who seemed to be holding up pretty well despite everything that had happened. "What do you think about Tech Guard?"

"I'm not sure." She shrugged. "I guess that depends on what was handed over in exchange for the cryptocurrency payment that Damien stole."

"Nina is all over that," Owens said. "She's tracking the payment to a bank in Budapest."

"Budapest?" Marsh scowled. "What on earth is in Budapest?"

"I can explain." A tall man dressed in a black suit walked into the house. He held up a cred pack. This time, he didn't flash it so fast it couldn't be examined. He held it steady.

Marsh glanced at Jackson, and they both stepped forward to examine the badge and accompanying ID closely.

They looked legit.

"My name is Paul Landry. I'm with the Department of

Defense." Landry turned to the second shorter man, who also held up his credentials for them to examine.

Marsh noticed that Captain Owens was using his phone to type a message, likely double-checking these guys as they were clearly the same ones who had shown up at the ranch.

"This is my partner, Terance Shaw. We've been tracking classified information being sold on the dark web. The most recent location of information that was purchased was to a buyer in Budapest."

"Classified information?" Marsh glanced at Damien's dad, who looked pale and shaken. "From this guy? Geoff Colter?"

"Actually, the target of our investigation was Dan Copeland, who we now know is Damien Colter." Landry looked directly at Stacy. "I'm sorry to say your husband used his computer hacking skills while working at Tech Guard to hack into the DOD database. The work was very similar to what he and his father did ten years ago."

"If that's true, why didn't you identify yourselves when you showed up at the Rocking T Ranch?" Marsh demanded. "We could have been working with you on this if we had known the Department of Defense was involved."

Landry shrugged, not looking the least bit apologetic. "We thought it was possible Ms. Copeland was a part of the hacking scheme. She has excellent computer skills, too, and we thought maybe they were working together on this venture. Besides, once Copeland was murdered, we didn't really know who to trust. We thought it was in our best interest to treat you as hostile until proven otherwise."

"Unbelievable," Marsh muttered. "Typical feds refusing to play nice."

"You can't blame us for being wary. It was a judgement call on our part. As it turned out, we trusted Harrington, which proved to be a problem. We decided to follow him to see if he could lead us to the father-and-son duo. We believe he was responsible for killing Damien." Terance Shaw glanced at Geoff. "We have our experts going through the video feed outside the ATM machine where he was murdered. The gunman was wearing a mask and gloves, but we're using other biological identifiers to see if the general description matches the US marshal."

"That idiot," Geoff said in disgust. "My stupid son must have reached out to Harrington. He must have thought he could somehow get immunity."

"No, we have reason to believe that you, Mr. Colter, led Harrington to your son," Landry said. "Because you and your son were a team in this hacking scheme. We think Harrington finally tracked you down. By the way, we found your apartment rented under the name of Harold Green. That's quite the computer setup you have there."

When Geoff paled and looked away, Marsh knew the DOD agents were correct. Father and son had reunited and gone back to their hacking days. He wasn't sure why Damien had stolen the cryptocurrency code. Maybe he'd had second thoughts about using the funds and hoped to turn everything over to the US Marshals Service. They may never know Damien's true intent. Bottom line was he'd been killed, leaving Geoff to spend time in prison for what they'd done.

"Does this mean Tech Guard as a company isn't involved?" Jackson asked, glancing from one fed to the other. "You think one of these guys managed to get inside to convince Matt Wade to get the computer from Stacy."

"Correct. We have no reason to suspect anyone else within Tech Guard is involved, but we have technical expert colleagues there now, interviewing the leadership team and taking control of their devices." A hint of a smile tugged at Landry's mouth. "They have some cameras in the facility, and we'll be combing through those video feeds to find who that person may have been."

From the way Geoff Colter's shoulders slumped, Marsh suspected he was the one who'd gotten inside to make the call to Matt Wade. It probably wasn't the first time Geoff had been inside the company. Damien may have shown him around the place.

"I'm sure we'll be able to put all the pieces together," Agent Shaw said, interrupting his thoughts. "Even if that means keeping Tech Guard shut down until our very thorough investigation is complete."

There was a long silence as they processed that information.

"Does this mean I can go home?" Stacy finally asked, her expression hopeful. "I really don't want to stay here any longer."

Landry and Shaw exchanged a long glance. "Yes, that's fine. We may have more questions for you," Landry said. "And we'll need that sonogram photo for evidence."

Stacy's eyes filled with tears at that. Marsh jumped to his feet. "No. You can get the code from our tech expert, Nina Hobson."

Landry scowled. "I'm afraid that's not good enough."

"Why not?" Marsh held the other man's gaze. "All you need is the code."

"Go ahead and take it." Stacy pushed the computer toward the agent. "I can ask the hospital to provide another image. I just want this to be over."

"Thank you." Landry stooped to snag the computer. "And I will get the device with the photo back to you without the code when we're finished."

"Yeah, whatever." Stacy wiped her tears away. "It's just a picture."

Of her baby! But Marsh held back the condemnation. The DOD agents were just doing their job. And he understood the chain of evidence was important. He rose and offered his hand to Stacy. "Let's go."

It took a few minutes for Marsh to get the SUV out of the garage and around the Jeep that had been driven by Colter, but soon they were on the highway. Stacy was quiet, not giving him any indication as to what she was thinking.

"I guess everything worked out the way it was supposed to," she finally said. "Damien is gone, his father will go to jail, and it sounds as if the government will find those who purchased the classified information."

"Yes, it's over for good." He reached for her hand. "I'm going to stay with you for a while. I'll sleep on the sofa," he quickly added when she turned to look at him. "I won't get in your way, but I don't want you to be alone."

She tightened her grip on his hand. "I was thinking that I might spend some time at the ranch. One of the perks of my job is that I can work remotely. No reason I can't stay at the Rocking T for a while. I know Tucker and Leanne won't mind."

Was that her way of avoiding him? His stomach knotted at the possibility she didn't share his feelings.

Ignoring his own despair, he understood Stacy needed to do what was best for herself, not for him or for anyone else. Her focus needed to be on her well-being and that of her baby.

He could wait for as long as it took.

"Okay, I'll take you to the ranch." He'd have taken her to the moon if he could. "But I'd still like to stay with you if that's okay. If nothing else, I can help with the ranch chores."

"Oh, Marsh." She squeezed his hand, and to his horror more tears filled her eyes. "That's more than okay. I'm so blessed that God brought you into my life."

"Really?" He pulled over to the side of the road, put the car in Park and turned in his seat to face her. "Stacy, I know you've been through a lot. But I want to spend more time with you. Maybe even attend your next doctor's appointment. If you'd like that," he hastened to add. "I'm not trying to invade your privacy, I just want to be there for you every step of the way. I can't bear the idea of you doing all of this alone."

"I'd love that." She released his hand to swipe at her eyes, then leaned over the center console to kiss his cheek. "I like spending time with you."

That admission made his heart race. He cupped his hand around her neck. "Stacy, I don't want to scare you, but I think I've fallen in love with you."

Her eyes widened, then she laughed. At first he was afraid she was laughing at him for being such a fool.

But then a bright smile lit up her face. "I'm not scared, Marsh. I'm thrilled. Because I love you, too."

Relief hit hard. He drew her in for a kiss but knew they couldn't linger. For one thing, sitting and kissing in the front seat of the car probably wasn't comfortable in her condition.

And secondly, he needed to talk to Tucker and fast. "Your brother is not going to be happy about this," he muttered as he released her.

"Don't be silly. Tucker won't mind." She patted his arm reassuringly. "He'll be happy that I'm happy."

"Yeah, maybe. I hope so." He leaned over to kiss her again, then put the car in drive and pulled back out into traffic.

"Marsh?" He glanced at her. "Do you believe God brought us together?"

"With all my heart," he agreed without hesitation. Because it was true. He couldn't imagine his future without Stacy and her daughter.

# EPILOGUE

*Four weeks later...*

Stacy couldn't believe how quickly Marsh had become integrated into her life. He'd been forced to take a full week off work after shooting and killing Noel Harrington while the DOD finished their investigation. But after he'd been cleared of any wrongdoing and he'd gone back to work, Marsh had made it a point to call and check on her almost daily.

There had been some adjusting on both sides. Her emotions sometimes got the better of her, and Marsh could be ridiculously overprotective.

But he was also sweet, kind and supportive. To her surprise, Tucker had not been enamored of the idea of her and Marsh seeing each other.

"Get over it, Tuck." She'd jabbed her finger into her brother's chest. "I'll date whoever I want. And Marsh is a hundred times better than anyone else out there. And you know that!"

"Yeah, yeah." Tucker rubbed the spot on his chest. "It's just that I want you to be happy, and being in a relationship with a Ranger isn't easy. Ask Leanne or Mari if you don't believe me."

"I love him." She'd narrowed her gaze. "I don't care if it's difficult. Most relationships have challenges. I love Marsh, so don't you dare scare him away."

After a long moment, Tucker had hugged her. "Okay, I hear you."

Now she paced the living room of the ranch, trying not to be impatient as she waited for Marsh to arrive. He'd claimed he needed to talk to her but had insisted they meet at the Rocking T.

It was, she thought with a smile, the first place they'd met. Way back in September when Tucker had saved Leanne's life.

Fitting that Marsh had saved hers, too.

When she saw the SUV rumble along the driveway, she relaxed. She knew Marsh's job meant he was in danger, just like Tucker, Sam and Jackson were. And that being with him would never be easy, as Tuck pointed out. But she loved him for the man he was. A pillar of strength and support.

Determined to put criminals behind bars.

When Marsh slid out from behind the wheel, she hurried out to meet him.

"Hey, beautiful." He grinned and swept her into his arms. "How are my two favorite girls today?"

"One is glad to see you, the other is too busy kicking me to notice you were gone." She pulled him into a long kiss. "I'm happy you're here."

"Me too. Seeing you is the highlight of my day." He held her close for a long moment, then stepped back. "Let's go inside."

She nodded, falling into step beside him. "Tucker and Leanne just got back from their hike. They're showering for dinner."

"Great." He smiled. "I'm starved."

"Pops made his infamous pot roast." She'd noticed her grandfather had been trying to do more around the house now that he'd fully recovered from his broken hip. But Pops wasn't as spry as he had been, which was why Tucker and Leanne had pretty much moved to the ranch full time. They'd offered for her to live there, too, after delivering her baby, but she hadn't made a decision yet about whether to sell the house.

When they made their way through the mudroom and into the kitchen, Stacy was surprised to see Tucker, Leanne and Pops all gathered around the island. "Wow, is dinner ready? I thought we had some time yet?"

"You ask me, you're running out of time, baby sis," Tucker teased. "You look ready to pop."

"I still have two months to go." Stacy glared at him. "And just so you know, if you say something like that to Leanne when she's at this stage of her pregnancy, she's likely to smack you."

"Agreed," Leanne said, jabbing her elbow into Tucker's side. "Don't even think about it."

"Excuse me, could I have your attention for a moment?" Marsh's comment took her by surprise.

She glanced at him, wondering what was up.

He stepped forward, took her hand and dropped to one knee. He pulled a ring from his pocket and presented it to her. "Stacy, will you please marry me? I promise to be the best husband possible to you and a good father to Ellie."

"Oh, Marsh, yes! Yes, I'll marry you." Tears filled

her eyes as he slipped the ring on her finger. Then he kissed her belly before rising to his feet and pulling her into his arms.

"How come you didn't ask me if it was okay to ask her to marry you?" Tucker asked with pretend annoyance.

"Because he asked me," Pops said. "And I gave him our blessing."

That surprised her, although it shouldn't have. Marsh had liked her old-fashioned name of Eleanor. She was touched that he'd cared enough to ask Pops for permission to marry her.

"Okay, Pops. You are the head of the household." Tucker grinned, then leaned in to kiss his own wife.

Stacy smiled at Marsh, then glanced at Pops, Tucker and Leanne. "My family," she whispered.

"Our family," Marsh corrected, placing a protective hand on her belly before kissing her again.

And she knew he was right. This was the family God had provided for them.

\* \* \* \* \*

*If you enjoyed this book, don't miss these other stories
from Laura Scott in her
Texas Justice miniseries:*

Texas Kidnapping Target
Texas Ranger Defender

*Available now from Love Inspired Suspense!
Find more great reads at LoveInspired.com*

Dear Reader,

Thanks so much for reading Marshall and Stacy's story in *Dangerous Texas Secrets*. This is the third book in my Texas Justice series, and I've really enjoyed writing about these wonderful Texas Rangers. And don't worry, I'm hard at work plotting Jackson's story. Hopefully that book will be out later this year.

I adore hearing from my readers! I can be found through my website at LauraScottbooks.com, via Facebook at LauraScottBooks, Instagram @laurascottbooks, and X @laurascottbooks. Please take a moment to subscribe to my YouTube channel at @LauraScottBooks-wr1xl.

Please consider taking a moment to sign up for my monthly newsletter on my website to learn about my upcoming books and special sales by my author friends. All subscribers receive a free novella.

Until next time...
*Laura Scott*

# Get up to 4 Free Books!

**We'll send you 2 free books from each series you try PLUS a free Mystery Gift.**

FREE
Value Over
**$25**

Both the **Love Inspired®** and **Love Inspired® Suspense** series feature compelling novels filled with inspirational romance, faith, forgiveness and hope.